Cooking with Memories

COOKING
W I T H
MEMORIES

Recipes and Recollections

LORA BRODY

THE STEPHEN GREENE PRESS
PELHAM BOOKS

THE STEPHEN GREENE PRESS/PELHAM BOOKS

Published by the Penguin Group
Viking Penguin, a division of Penguin Books USA Inc., 40 West 23rd Street,
    New York, New York 10010, U.S.A.
Penguin Books Ltd., 27 Wrights Lane, London W8 5TZ, England
Penguin Books Australia Ltd, Ringwood, Victoria, Australia
Penguin Books Canada Ltd, 2801 John Street, Markham, Ontario,
    Canada L3R 1B4
Penguin Books (N.Z.) Ltd, 182–190 Wairau Road, Auckland 10,
    New Zealand

Penguin Books Ltd, Registered Offices: Harmondsworth, Middlesex,
    England

First published in 1989 by The Stephen Greene Press/Pelham Books
Distributed by Viking Penguin, a division of Penguin Books USA Inc.

10 9 8 7 6 5 4 3 2 1

Library of Congress Cataloging-in-Publication Data
Brody, Lora, 1945–
    Cooking with memories : recipes & recollections / by Lora Brody.
        p. cm.
    Includes index.
    ISBN 0-8289-0667-X
    1. Cookery. I. Title.
TX714.B77   1989
641.5--dc20   89-32591
                                                                   CIP

Designed by Deborah Schneider
Set in Administer by CopyRight, Bedford MA
Printed in the United States of America
Produced by Unicorn Production Services, Inc.

Contents

Introduction
xi

Breaking the Fast
1

Get Well Food
17

The Toni Girl
31

Chips
41

Thanksgiving
50

Reading at the Table
57

Down the Beach: The Sand Castle Years
68

Doughnuts and Coppertone
75

Canning Wars
83

Force-Feeding
94

Pile on the Gelt
97

Baked Potatoes
103

Casseroles—or What Are You Trying to Hide?
109

Good-bye
119

Hello
134

Shooting Stars
143

The Ladies' Nostalgia Dinner
150

Springerle
162

Fried Chicken
168

Smooth Food
180

Gourmet Chicken Soup?
191

The Velveeta Cook-Off
201

Glossary
207

Index
209

*This book is dedicated
to my mother,
Millie Apter*

I place in position before my mind's eye the still recent taste of that first mouthful, and I feel something start within me, something that leaves its resting-place and attempts to rise, something that has been embedded like an anchor at a great depth; I do not know yet what it is, but I can feel it mounting slowly: I can measure the resistance, I can hear the echo of great spaces traversed.

MARCEL PROUST
Remembrance of Things Past

Introduction

Two women enter a kitchen. One immediately notices the design, the layout, the colors of the counters, the quality of the cabinets and appliances, the sources of light. The other woman notices only what's cooking. Stew can be simmering in a hundred-dollar copper kettle custom designed in Paris or in a cheap aluminum pan from the hardware store—the vessel is inconsequential—the smell is everything. For that second woman the simmering fragrance of meat and wine and stock and herbs doesn't simply register in the present, it flings open the doors of yesterdays and other kitchens when other stews bubbled and other kitchens smelled as welcoming; it stirs a string of memories, smells, and tastes from places far away, from home and from childhood. I, of course, am the second woman.

For a very long time I was unable to pinpoint from exactly what source the energy and imagination and drive to work with food had come to me. People often grilled me: "What made you decide to cook for a living?" "Did your mother (grandmother, aunt) inspire you?" "Where did you study, learn, train?" There was no simple answer to these questions, so I would toss off a shrug and a slippery, "I dunno," and leave it at that.

Their wondering got me wondering though (and I never really liked that coy answer anyway), so I set about looking back, remembering the beginnings. This book is the result. These stories are the steps, the paths, and the passages that took a kid who would rather read than eat to a woman whose life is full and overflowing with the flavors and smells and textures of good things to cook and eat.

For me, the spark of memory kindled by tastes, textures, or aromas illuminated long-forgotten episodes; funny, poignant, tender, and treasured. And it worked both ways. As the memories were called up, along with them came the recipes, recorded on yellowed and dog-eared index cards, scribbled on the flyleaves of old cookbooks, buried in the saved letters of friends. I resurrected treasured dishes, some of which had not seen the light of day since 1957, and found that my children loved them as much as I had. The passage continues.

The ultimate pleasure that comes from cooking with memories is that now I have a real answer to the question: where did it all start?

While I do not keep kosher in my house, I appreciate that some of the people cooking from this book do. In each recipe I have attempted to offer substitutions that will accommodate the kosher cook.

Breaking the Fast

There is a certain part of the Yom Kippur service that, in traditional synagogues, children usually do not stay to watch or hear. During this Yizkor service the grown-ups remember relatives and close friends who have died, calling out their names to keep their memories alive. There are two reasons that the children are ushered out by mothers who are dressed for the solemn holiday in new fall outfits often too warm for the Indian summer day. The first is a superstition that says that if one says the Kaddish (memorial service for the dead) without having lost a loved one, then you are baiting the evil eye. The second reason is that back when I was a little girl parents didn't let their children see them cry. The presence of all those sweet and innocent faces, as yet untouched by the grief that loss can bring, would inhibit and divide the loyalties of the mourners, and the true business of this difficult portion of the service would not get done. I remember the first time my son Jonathan was allowed to stay for Yizkor. It was the year of his Bar Mitzvah so he was thirteen. In our shul each person rises, one after the other, and says the name of a departed loved one and, if they wish, something about them. I felt it was a coming of age—for both us—to have him see his mother stand and be overwhelmed with the sadness of remembrance.

The solemnity and almost exhausting seriousness of Yom Kippur, the Day of Atonement and repentance when Jews ask, through prayer and fasting, God's forgiveness for sins and transgressions of the year gone by, was hard for a child to endure, especially since it followed the joyousness of Rosh Hashanah, which celebrates the Jewish new year. The hardness of the wooden benches was barely relieved by the red velvet cushions covering them, since their stuffings were well flattened from years of use. If you weren't careful how you sat down after each passage that required standing up (and those were many indeed), you ended up with a worn velvet-covered button making a painful dent in your backside. The air in the sanctuary never stirred. It grew warmer and heavier each passing hour with the feeling of the mass of packed bodies rocking back and forth to prayers (gently or rather violently each in their own style) chanted in unfamiliar special Yom Kippur melodies. Even the light that filtered in through the high bank of stained glass windows seemed weighted, as if it was passing only through the somber greens and murky browns instead of the reds and orange-yellows that could make the windows seem, on occasion, like a luminous living thing.

The service, even with the Yizkor break, seemed never-ending, and the fidgeting that went on in the female subteen set was directly proportional to two things: if you were old enough to wear stockings and had a garter belt digging into the back of your thighs, and how long you had been fasting. The boys fidgeted no matter what, and if the weather outside was gorgeous, they were like rabbits on uppers, dying to hop away to roll in piles of newly raked leaves and tune in to see if the Dodgers were winning the Series. Since I never seemed old enough to wear stockings and I had a fantasy life active enough to get me through most of the four-plus hours of the morning service, all I had to contend with was a hollow, grumbling stomach. Although this was the wrong place for it, I suppose, I used my holier-than-thou attitude to conquer my hunger. It was the need to feel more grown-up than those other kids that kept me pure. Also, my cousins and I were determined to out-fast one another, and I'd be damned if I would break the fast before they did. The thing that really kept me going, however, was looking forward to my yearly walk with Rose.

My Aunt Rose and I had established a special Yom Kippur tradition that helped us pass those endless afternoon hours between the end of the morning service and sundown, which was when one could break the long fast that began with sundown the night before. We walked from her house on Magnolia Street in Hartford's North End to my house on Canaan Street near the Bloomfield line. This was a distance of about four miles.

Our route never varied; it took us down Albany Avenue past the drugstore (where I longingly thought of the rack of Wise's potato chips—I would have killed for just a nibble), skirting the Lenox Theater—fortunately closed for the holiday since the smell of popcorn would have done me in. Down Vine Street past my old elementary school (where the third grade teacher made the kids who wet their pants sit on the radiator until they and their pants dried) and toward Rockville Street, where my parents had moved after they left Magnolia Street. My few memories of the Rockville Street apartment included my father singing us to sleep with "Old Man River" (in such a deep, bass voice) and my mother complaining bitterly about having to climb three flights of stairs with two little babies, a heavy stroller, and heavy bags of groceries. That's why they moved to a ranch house after that. From Rockville Street we turned into Kenney Park, where some of the families from our synagogue were strolling in their holiday finery waiting out the remaining hours until the start of the late afternoon service signaling the end of the holiday.

My usual rambunctious style of walking was subdued both from hunger and the company of my aunt, who was not given to jumping over cracks (break your mother's back) or trying to leapfrog over fire hydrants. As we ambled toward my house I savored the deliciously illegal feeling of being out of school on a perfectly gorgeous fall afternoon, dressed to kill (that unmercifully itchy crinoline slip that made the skirt of my green-and-blue plaid taffeta dress stick out and swish so smartly was, in fact, killing me), walking with my aunt while other kids sat in stuffy study halls considering the mysteries of algebra or in science lab pondering the inner workings of a rat pickled in formaldehyde. I relished the sweet taste of freedom of having been sprung not only from school but from the morning's long ordeal in the synagogue. Hadn't I more than earned it by sitting still for four and a half hours?

As the sun began to dip lower in the sky and the breeze picked up, autumn-painted leaves swirled around our feet and drifted down from the old maples and elms in lazy swoops like undirected rainbowed tissue paper airplanes. The closer we got to my house the more the conversation turned to the meal that was awaiting us there.

"Mom made four dozen rugelach the night before last," I told Rose, my mouth aching at the thought of those tender little crescent cookies laden with walnuts and raisins.

"You're not going to break your fast with rugelach. Don't you want a cup of borscht first?" My mouth watered furiously at the thought of the ruby red liquid, thick with onions and chunks of beets.

"Yes, borscht first with lots of sour cream on top." My stomach was grumbling very loudly. "Then herring salad—or maybe kugel." Oh God—my mother's potato kugel served with a spoonful of her homemade raspberry applesauce—my knees were beginning to feel rubbery.

We were approaching the last leg of the walk—the long hill from Blue Hills Avenue down Tower Avenue toward Canaan Street—when Rose said the fatal word: "Blintzes...did your mother say she was making blintzes?" Rose asked innocently. Just the thought of them made me want to sit down on the sidewalk and weep. Fat buttery pillows of warm squooshy cheese slathered with my mom's exquisite blueberry sauce and topped (of course) with sour cream. Sour cream was a major theme in our break-fast meal; the center of the dining room table would feature a cut crystal bowl filled to the brim with sliced bananas mixed with sour cream accompanied by a smaller crystal dish of dark brown sugar to sprinkle on top. Positioned around this bowl like so many of Jupiter's moons orbited other bowls filled with salmon salad, spears of sour pickles, platters of sliced tomatoes from the garden, and rings of Bermuda onion. On a large cutting board would wait a giant-sized challa and a black bread with the paper label still glued to the side ready to be anointed with sweet whipped butter. There would be a steaming pot of kasha varnishkes for my father (I didn't learn to love the combination of bow tie noodles and buckwheat until I was a grown-up).

Almost home we passed other families walking with slightly renewed vigor toward their homes and the promise of the delicious meals that waited there. It was usually at this point that my aunt reminded me about people who were always hungry (usually these were people in China, for some reason), people who never had enough to eat. And here I was thinking that I could barely live through one day without food. I would spend the last few blocks walking hand in hand with my aunt who loved and fed me unconditionally, somberly reflecting about how lucky I was that I didn't live in China.

My mother's house was warm and alive with subdued but relieved people happy to have this long day over, and it was permeated with wonderfully promising smells. My cousins and I made my brother run back and forth from the porch to the living room to report the southern progress of the sun toward Avon Mountain. I snuck into the kitchen to survey the desserts stored securely in their Tupperware containers. There were thick slices of dark, moist honey cake, which my mother made with buckwheat honey and strong coffee; a babka studded with brandy-soaked golden raisins; and tiny cherry- and cheese-filled Danish that the New York cousins brought with them. Cooling on top of the stove was my Aunt Bea's famous brandied bread pudding. It took a few moments of struggling with those determined-to-stick lids, but just as soon as my brother called out the good news, I was ready. I shut my eyes and bit into a rugelach. It was a perfectly heavenly reward, made even more delicious by the fast that preceded it.

Rugelach

Beware—you can't eat just one!

FOR THE DOUGH

2 sticks (½ pound) sweet (unsalted) butter, at room temperature
8 ounces cream cheese, at room temperature

¼ cup sugar
1 teaspoon vanilla
2 cups flour, measured after sifting

Cream the butter and cream cheese, mix in the sugar and vanilla. Mix in the flour and form the dough into a smooth ball. Divide the dough into 4 portions and cover each with plastic wrap and refrigerate for several hours.

FOR THE FILLING

1 cup granulated sugar
½ cup brown sugar, firmly packed
1 teaspoon cinnamon

1½ cups golden raisins
1½ cups walnuts, coarsely chopped

Combine all the ingredients and stir well.

TO ASSEMBLE

1 12-ounce (1½ cups) jar apricot preserves, heated
¼ cup milk

2 tablespoons sugar mixed with 1 teaspoon cinnamon

Remove the dough from the refrigerator and let it sit on the counter for 15 minutes before using.

Preheat the oven to 350 degrees with the rack in the center position. Line three heavy-duty baking sheets with parchment, or butter each sheet and dust it with flour, knocking off the excess flour.

One at a time roll out each dough portion, on a lightly floured board, into a 9-inch circle ⅛ inch thick. Cut the dough into 12 triangles or pieces of "pie." With a thin knife loosen the triangles and coat one side with a thin layer of apricot preserves (a small teaspoon is good for this job).

Spread a generous amount of the raisin-nut filling down the entire length and width of each triangle. Press the filling firmly with your fingertips and, starting with the wide end, roll the triangle up and bend the ends around to form a slight crescent shape.

Place the rugelach about 1½ inches apart on the prepared baking sheet. Brush with milk and then sprinkle with the cinnamon sugar. Bake for 16-18 minutes or until lightly browned.

Makes 4 dozen

Herring Salad

1 large (32 ounces) jar
   herring snacks—found
   in your supermarket
   refrigerated section
1 hard (stale) roll or slice of
   stale white bread
¼ cup cider vinegar
1 medium purple onion,
   cut in chunks

2 medium or 1 large stalk
   celery, sliced in 1-inch pieces
1 Granny Smith apple, peeled,
   cored, and quartered
1 hard-boiled egg
1 tablespoon sugar

Drain the juice off the herring snacks and discard. Break up the roll or bread and soak it in the vinegar. In the work bowl of a food processor process the onion, celery, and apple on and off for 2 or 3 seconds each time. Add the egg, process for 5 seconds, then add the herring, the roll, the vinegar, and sugar, and process off and on only until incorporated but not pureed. The consistency should be coarse.

Serve on pumpernickel bread or crackers.

Makes 5 cups

Cold (Meatless) Borscht

2 large bunches of beets
  (about 3 pounds), peeled
  and grated
2½ quarts water
1 medium onion, finely diced
2 stalks celery, diced
½ cup fresh dill or
  1 tablespoon dried dill

2 tablespoons salt
2 teaspoons sour salt or
  juice of one medium lemon
¾ cup sugar, or to taste
salt and pepper to taste
sliced boiled potato or
  sour cream for garnish

In a large soup pot combine the beets, water, onion, celery, dill, salt, sour salt or lemon juice and half the sugar. Bring to a boil and simmer uncovered for 20 minutes or until the beets are very tender. Add more sugar if necessary. Serve hot or cold topped with the boiled potato or a dollop of sour cream.

Serves 8–10

FOR CREAMY BORSCHT

To the above recipe add:

3 eggs that have been beaten together with one pint of sour cream in a large bowl. Whisking constantly, very gradually mix in 2 cups of the hot borscht. Stir the rest of the egg mixture into the remaining soup. Simmer only until hot, stirring constantly — *do not boil!* Season with salt and pepper and serve hot or cold and serve with a dollop of sour cream.

Serves 8–10

Kasha Varnishkes

---

1 cup coarsely granulated kasha
1 egg, beaten
2 cups chicken, beef, or vegetable stock (canned or homemade or made with a bouillon cube)
1 teaspoon salt (if you use commercial stock, which tends to be salty, add the salt at the very end)
½ teaspoon white pepper
3 tablespoons butter or margarine
2 large onions, chopped
¼ cup vegetable oil
8 ounces cooked and drained bow tie egg noodles

Combine the kasha with the beaten egg, making sure all the grains are well moistened. Place the kasha in a large frying pan set over medium heat and cook, stirring frequently until the egg has dried.

Bring the stock, salt, pepper, and butter or margarine to a boil. Add the liquid to the cooked kasha, stir gently, and then cover and cook over low heat for 15 minutes. Remove the cover and fluff the grains with a fork. If the grains are very moist, cover and continue cooking for another few minutes.

Sauté the onion in the oil until lightly browned. Combine the kasha, the onions, and the noodles. Serve hot, cold, or at room temperature.

Serves 10

Potato Kugel

2 tablespoons vegetable oil
5 pounds Idaho potatoes,
  peeled
1 large onion
3 extra large eggs, slightly
  beaten

¼ cup vegetable oil
2 tablespoons matzo meal
2 teaspoons baking powder
¼ cup boiling water
2 teaspoons salt, or to taste
Freshly ground pepper to taste

Preheat the oven to 375 degrees. Place the 2 tablespoons of oil in a large ovenproof baking dish. Place this in the oven to heat while you assemble the kugel.

Grate the potatoes either by hand or in a food processor. Drain the liquid off, reserving it. Combine the potatoes, onion, eggs, and ¼ cup oil. Mix together the meal and baking powder and add to the potatoes, mixing very well.

Pour the water off the reserved potato liquid, add ¼ cup boiling water to the remaining starch, and mix well. Add to the potato mixture. Add the salt and pepper.

Pour into the hot dish in the oven and bake 1 hour until well browned.

Serves 8–10

Brandied Bread Pudding

This fabulously rich and deliciously satisfying concoction has a crispy top layer, a creamy inside, and a buttery sweet brandied topping. It is perfect for brunch, for dessert after a light meal, or for any special occasion that calls for a memorable dish. It can be made and baked several days ahead of time, then refrigerated until time to reheat and add the topping. I have doubled and even tripled the recipe for a large crowd. Since it is so very rich count on one recipe feeding at least twelve people. Leftovers heat up beautifully in the oven or in the microwave. I make mine in an oval glass baking dish, although any dish with at least two-inch-high sides is fine.

This recipe calls for stale croissants. Economically it is better to buy them at half-price from your local bakery; if you can't do this, buy the croissants at least two days before you plan to make the bread pudding and leave them uncovered on a counter or table on cake racks (so the bottoms get stale as well).

FOR THE BREAD PUDDING

2 tablespoons soft butter (for greasing the pan)	½ cup brandy
Approximately 1 dozen stale plain croissants	6 extra large eggs
5 cups light cream	1⅓ cups sugar
1 stick (4 ounces) sweet butter at room temperature, cut into pieces	Pinch of salt
	2 teaspoons vanilla

Use the softened butter to generously grease a 9 × 13-inch Pyrex ovenproof baking dish or an oval dish of approximately the same size that has at least 2-inch-high sides. Slice the croissants top to bottom so that you have about 7–8 ½-inch slices per croissant. Layer the slices, slightly overlapping in the buttered pan. You will have enough slices to make several layers, making the center slightly higher than the sides.

Set a fine mesh metal strainer in a bowl big enough to hold the cream and eggs combined. In a 2-quart saucepan combine the light cream, the butter, and the brandy. Heat until the butter melts and the cream is scalded (small bubbles will appear around the edge of the pan). While the cream is heating mix the eggs, sugar, and salt in an electric mixer or by hand with a wire whisk. Pour about ⅓ of the hot cream into the egg mixture, mix well, and return the egg/cream mixture to the pan. Cook over low heat, stirring constantly with a rubber spatula until the mixture starts to thicken slightly. Immediately pour the mixture through the strainer. Stir in the vanilla. Carefully pour the mixture on top of the croissant slices. Cover the dish with plastic wrap and refrigerate for at least 3 hours. This allows the croissants to soak up the custard.

Preheat the oven to 350 degrees with the rack in the center position. Remove the plastic wrap and bake the bread pudding for 45–50 minutes or until the top has turned golden brown. If you find that the top is browning too fast, cover the dish loosely with foil. While the pudding is baking prepare the topping.

FOR THE TOPPING

1 cup brown sugar
¼ cup molasses
3 tablespoons brandy

4 tablespoons butter
½ cup orange juice

Combine all the ingredients. Remove the pudding from the oven and let sit for 5–10 minutes. Then cook the topping, stirring constantly, until the sugar has melted and the mixture is smooth. Pour over the pudding and serve.

Serves 12

Cheese Blintzes with Blueberry Sauce

FOR THE CREPES

1 cup flour, measured after sifting	1 tablespoon vegetable oil
	¼ teaspoon salt
1 cup whole milk	1 tablespoon sugar
3 extra large eggs	1 teaspoon butter

Place the first 6 ingredients in the work bowl of a blender or food processor, blend or process for 30 seconds or until very well mixed (scrape down the sides several times), and then transfer to a container or pitcher with a pourable spout.

In a small nonstick shallow sauté pan or crepe pan set over medium heat, melt the butter until it is bubbling and very slightly brown. Pour in just enough batter to coat the bottom of the pan. Cook for about 1 minute, then pour off the excess batter, leaving a lip on the side of the pan. Continue cooking for another 2 minutes or until the crepe starts pulling away from the sides of the pan and the top is dry. Place the crepe on a plate to cool. Repeat until all the batter is used up, placing wax paper between the crepes to keep them from sticking together and adding a little more butter to the pan and waiting for it to heat with each new crepe (this step is not necessary if you use a nonstick pan).

The crepes can be frozen after they are completely cooled, if desired.

FOR THE FILLING

8 ounces cream cheese	¾ cup sugar
1 pound farmer cheese	2 tablespoons sour cream

Combine all the ingredients, beating only until well mixed and creamy. Do not overbeat because this will make the filling runny.

FOR THE BLUEBERRY SAUCE

1 quart blueberries, fresh or frozen	1 tablespoon instant tapioca
	Juice of 1 lemon
⅓ cup sugar	

Place the blueberries in a medium-sized saucepan and sprinkle the sugar over them. Sprinkle in the tapioca and add the lemon juice. Toss the berries and let them sit for 15 minutes. Cook over low heat, stirring constantly, until the berries give up their juices and begin to thicken. Cool slightly before serving.

TO ASSEMBLE AND SERVE THE BLINTZES

2 tablespoons oil	Cinnamon sugar
1 tablespoon butter	Sour cream

Take 1 crepe and set it on the work space with the lip closest to you. Place 2 teaspoons of filling just above the lip. Roll the lip over the filling, roll once, tuck in each side, and continue rolling until you have a neat package. Finish with the seam side down. Continue until all the blintzes have been formed.

In a large sauté pan set over medium heat melt oil and butter until hot. Cook several blintzes at a time (taking care not to crowd them in the pan) for 5 minutes on each side or until they are golden brown.

Serve the blintzes hot and pass the blueberry sauce, cinnamon sugar, and sour cream separately.

Makes between 12 and 16 blintzes depending on the size of your crepe pan

Aunt Bessie's Babka

My mother's Aunt Bessie Citron is a baker without equal. Among her many triumphs is this melt-in-your-mouth sour cream coffee cake, simply known as Bessie's Babka.

2 sticks (½ pound) sweet (unsalted) butter
½ cup sugar
1 cup sour cream
1 package granulated yeast (½ ounce)
4 extra large eggs
4½ cups flour, measured after sifting
½ teaspoon salt

4 tablespoons sweet butter, softened
½ cup ground walnuts or pecans
½ cup golden raisins
1 egg yolk
2 tablespoons water
2 tablespoons sugar mixed with 2 teaspoons cinnamon

Melt the butter and place it in a mixing bowl. Add the sugar and mix well. Mix in the sour cream, the yeast, and the eggs, one at a time. When this mixture is well combined stir in the flour and salt, mixing until the flour is well incorporated. Cover the bowl with plastic wrap and refrigerate overnight.

Preheat the oven to 375 degrees and grease 2 heavy-duty cookie sheets. Divide the dough into 4 pieces and on a lightly floured board roll each one into a 9-inch rectangle. Smear each rectangle with a tablespoon of softened butter, sprinkle with the ground nuts, some raisins, and roll into a cylinder. Place 2 rolls on each cookie sheet about 4 inches apart and paint with an egg wash made of 1 egg yolk and 2 tablespoons water. Sprinkle with the cinnamon sugar. Bake for 30–35 minutes. This is delicious served warm, or it can be cooled completely, frozen, and reheated.

Makes 4 babkas

Get Well Food

I tolerated school until the third grade. Kindergarten was undemanding and you got to color and cut and paste a lot, which was fine with me. First and second grades weren't terribly strenuous either since I had learned to read at home and could spend most of my time daydreaming while the other kids learned their letters. Numbers were a drag but not impossible. . .yet.

I took one look around the first day of third grade and saw the writing on the wall. School suddenly meant work. It meant wearing dresses instead of pants. It meant being neat and quiet and obedient. It meant that boys acted dumb toward the pretty girls and the pretty girls seemed to love it. Not being a pretty girl, I was pretty confused and disgusted by the whole thing. It meant a change in command from my warm and patient motherly teachers to this spinsterly witch who wanted you to sit with your hands clasped on your desk and say ''Yes, Ma'am''; who didn't give a hoot if the waistband of your slip was cutting off your circulation; wouldn't let you go to the bathroom until lunchtime; and who, in an effort to get me to switch from being left-handed to being right-handed, threatened to tie my good hand behind my back during writing lessons (all the while admonishing the other students to learn from my example).

I hated her and I hated school. An ice cube started to form somewhere in my middle, and every day it grew a little colder and a little bigger. It was about the time I saw her make Spencer McGovern sit on the radiator because he had wet his pants that the ice cube turned into a stomachache. It was also about the time that the world had seen the very last of Indian summer for that year, and the chilly, chapped hand of November was pulling down the dark shades of winter. No more leaves to kick on the long walk to school, a freezing cold wind whipping my skirt up, and the mean boys next door discovering how scared I got when they threatened to put gum in my hair and push me into the gutter. After two months I had had enough of school. Stomachaches seemed the most sensible way out.

My mother must have hated school too, because it wasn't terribly hard to convince her that I was in terrible pain and needed to stay in bed. Since I carried that ice cube of school anxiety around with me constantly, I could call on it to get me out of school. I started my routine at breakfast, since I figured that by getting dressed and ready for school I had demonstrated the best of intentions. At the table I would fix my eye on my juice glass, scrunch my eyes closed, wrap my arms around my middle, and rock very gently back and forth. If someone didn't notice right away, I would rock with a bit more aggression, working into near epileptic frenzy (all the while watching my mother's reaction out of the corner of my eye).

"She's faking again," my brother never hesitated to point out, at which point I would start the moaning segment of the act. "Ohhhh... my stomach...I'm dying...the pain...."

Too much Loretta Young infused into this drama. My mother would roll her eyes, place her hand on my head, and order me to the bathroom to try to "work things through," where I would leave the door ajar so my distress call could still be heard. Ultimately I was given the go-ahead, and with ill-disguised glee I would shoot my brother a smug victorious sneer and head with light heart back to bed.

As glorious as these reprieves were, since my mother and I both knew what was up, I was pretty much ignored after my brother left for school and my mother did her housework. Boredom and a vague feeling of guilt at having pulled one over on my mom conspired to make my day at home only marginally better than one at school. I was much happier, although certainly more uncomfortable (at least at first), to earn the right to stay home when I was really sick.

My first justifiable long siege came with the onset of mumps. I remember sitting in the overheated, underventilated classroom watching the winter wind blow the last of the oak leaves off the branches. Several pigeons huddled miserably on the ledge near the window, their dirty gray feathers ruffled by the bone-chilling

November gusts. They must have known the worst was yet to come. I felt gloomy. Staring out the window at the dark gray sky only made me feel worse. Rain lashed against the trees and streamed down the windows. So much for outdoor recess and my beloved kickball—the high point of the day.

Focusing my attention away from the lesson and directly on the window, I began to make mental bets on which raindrop would make it to the bottom first and be turned into the tiny river running along the sill. I found I could approximate the raindrops on my work sheet if I dipped my pen in the ink well and gouged the paper with the loaded nib. I didn't see the witch quietly making her way toward the back of my desk. With no warning I was grabbed from behind and propelled, my shoulder in her viselike grip, to the front of the room.

The teacher yelled about my not paying attention, about staring out the window, about messing up my paper, about my attitude in general. She still had me in her grip so I couldn't back up before I threw up on her shoes. Sensibly, she let go at that point and sent me down to the nurse, who took a look at my flushed red cheeks, felt my warm forehead, and called my mother.

As I snuggled next to my mother in the car on the way home, I luxuriated in the chills that were making my skin feel like it was imbued with extra nerve endings that tingled alternately hot and cold. There was the deep feeling of relief in the knowledge that not only did I get to go home in the middle of the morning, but after my performance starring the teacher's shoes, I would never have to go back to school again.

"Mumps," said the pediatrician, shaking down his thermometer. "She'll be in bed for at least ten days, I'm afraid." He looked like he felt sorry for me. Well, he could save his pity. I was in heaven.

Outside the rain had changed to driving snow. The other kids would be practicing the Palmer method; endless concentric circles on yellow lined paper. (My pencil was never sharp enough and my circles, smudged from my left hand's backhand journey across them, fell in on top of each other like a fallen stack of hula hoops. The teacher always wrote, "NOT YOUR BEST EFFORT" on my papers.) Then those same kids would have to trudge home for lunch through icy puddles, the slush spraying down the backs of their boots, only to face the return trip for the afternoon session. Meanwhile here I was, basking in the yellow glow of the lamp from my parents' dresser.

When I was really sick, I got to stay in my parents' four-poster bed until the evening, when my father would carry me back into my own bed. My mother helped me change into a warm flannel nightgown and tucked me in between the cool sheets. She gave me some Aspergum to chew on and wrapped a warm towel around my neck. I didn't feel really sick at this point so she put a couple of pillows behind my head and brought me a stack of books. Moments later the delicious smell of soup wafted out of the kitchen toward my empty stomach. The buttery vegetable broth glided down my throat and infused my whole being with an inner glow.

That was the last thing I was able to eat for several days, because as those of you who were born before there was a mumps vaccine may remember, the first several days are an agony of sore and swollen throat, headaches, and fever. The nights had a nightmarish quality. It was hard to tell what was real in my parents' room. The big maple dresser became a boogeyman, and in the viney rose pattern of the wallpaper I saw grotesque goblin faces and bizarre mutilated animals. My throat was so sore I could hardly swallow, and the fever left me with chills that quickly became waves of fire. My mother kept cool washcloths on my head and always knew when they needed to be changed. Her cool, dry hands seemed to draw the heat out of my flaming face. The first few nights she and my father took turns rubbing me down with witch hazel, the smell of which was so distinctive that to this day when I open a bottle of the stuff, I am zoomed back to my parents' bed, lying loosely wrapped in a flannel sheet, feeling the thin, pungent liquid evaporating off my skin.

Mornings were my best time, after my mother had taken away the sweat-soaked sheets and replaced them with smooth, dry fresh ones. The accumulated brightness outside hurt my eyes, so the blinds were drawn against the reflected snow light. After the first bad days I was able to sip, from a large tablespoon, lukewarm tea spiked with honey and lemon. I didn't feel like doing anything but watching the snow drift and swirl around my brother, who was busy constructing a giant snow fort in the yard. The irony that all the other kids were free from school because of the snow (and without the mumps) did not escape me.

Close to noon my grandmother arrived, having walked the near-mile to our place. She looked like one of those jolly Polish peasants on the cover of *National Geographic*, cheeks whipped to scarlet from the winter gusts, wrapped in her long overcoat and crowned with a flowing black-and-red-fringed babushka. Her galoshes were frosted in white and her breath was labored after the three-flight climb to our apartment. Not even bothering to take off her coat she made a beeline to where, tired of the view from the bedroom, I languished on the living room sofa. She extracted a teacup from a plastic bag, pulled off the wax paper that was held with a piece of string, and pronounced the cure-all, "Junket!" She held it close to my face. Her hands smelled of the onions she had fried in chicken fat for my grandfather's lunch. I took one look at the insipid yellow disk molded inside the bottom of the cup and had a flashback of the teacher's shoes. "Ma...please don't make me eat that stuff," I wheezed.

"Mater (that's what I called my grandmother, an affectation from her Liverpool days) made that special for you and walked all the way over here in the storm to bring it. The least you could do is try."

"What's in it? It looks like custard and I hate custard," I demanded hoarsely.

"Just try a little." They wouldn't tell me the ingredients—a very bad sign. I clamped my mouth down tight and tried to turn my head away but was hampered by my glands, which had filled my poor neck out and made me look like Winston Churchill with a goiter.

"It will make your throat feel better. Maybe afterward you could listen to the radio." Here was a bribe that could move me. I had forgotten about my radio friends waiting to entertain me and take my mind off my woes.

"OK, I'll try a tiny tiny bit and if I don't like it, that's it. What's that brown stuff on top?"

"A little grated nutmeg." Oh, great. Custard with weird spices on top. If I wasn't feeling rotten before, this would probably kill me.

My mother slid the spoon into the junket and scooped up a neat crescent, which she aimed toward my mouth. My throat constricted at the very thought of anything traveling through it. My grandmother and my mother both opened their mouths wide in anticipation as the spoon moved nearer my lips. Monkey see, monkey do, huh? This monkey opened her mouth the tiniest crack and my mother jammed the spoon in. The bland sweetness coated my tongue and signaled to my throat to relax since, upon entering my mouth the junket was less solid than it appeared, it wouldn't hurt going down. My empty stomach responded by signaling for more. Another spoonful was deposited. I ran the nutmeg between my tongue and the roof of my mouth and tiny sparks of flavor were set free. The silky semiliquid soothed my throat like my mother's cool hand stroking my forehead. My grandmother oversaw my mother's ministrations until every bit of junket was gone.

As promised, I got the radio. It was a square brown wooden box about a foot and a half long and a foot high, with two brown plastic knobs on the front on either side of a cloth-covered area where the sound came from. When you turned the knob on the left, a dim yellow light emanated from the dial and a very faint whine indicated that things were warming up inside. Since we only listened to one station, I didn't have to bother fiddling to tune in my favorite programs. The same station that brought us Bob Steel's breakfast club every morning (if you ate all your breakfast your mother could call in and have Bob Steel say your name on the Clean Plate Club Hall of Fame segment of the show—I never came close to finishing my breakfast and hated Bob Steel for not recognizing those of us who simply couldn't go the distance).

That brown box with its varnish long worn off from my absent-minded caressing was my magic escape machine. The pain in my muscles and the ache in my throat faded as Helen Trent's dilemmas wafted over the airwaves. Can a woman over forty find happiness with a man. . .Our Gal Sunday, Ma Perkins. . .radio families, friends, and relatives came and went into my sickroom, bringing tears, laughter, and drama so believable (to me) that I surely expected my father to come home each night, fling his paper, hat, and briefcase on the sofa, dance my mother around the room, and announce that we were moving to the Arctic, where he had taken a job as a forest ranger. Listening to the radio rekindled my appetite, because interspersed with commercial jingles extolling the virtues of Bon Ami cleanser and Ivory Flakes (pure as the driven snow) were mouth-watering and stomach-grumbling plugs for Campbell's soup (Mmmm Mmmmm good). My mother (the mind reader) would show up at my bedroom door around noon, tray in hand, bearing tomato soup and saltines. In a few minutes both the bowl and I had a red mustache and life seemed worth living again. During the afternoons I drifted off to Stella Dallas while the snow turned to slush outside and the saltine crumbs in my bed made me dream of sand in my bathing suit on a hot July day at the beach.

When my father came home at night he didn't break any big news about a career change or dance my mother around the kitchen. He did, however, patiently review my newly reorganized collection of dog-eared trading cards (kittens with kittens, puppies with puppies) and sit with me while we listened to the radio about news from Korea. I even got him to submit to a game or two of Chinese checkers. I was in heaven; safe and secure in the bosom of my family, loved and understood and far, far away from the scary world of third grade and the evil witch who presided over it.

After a week of junket, soup, and slices of oranges I was ready to move back toward more substantial food. My mother made egg in the nest, a soft poached egg served atop a thick slice of challa; French toast slathered in maple syrup and melted butter; and green pea soup with chunks of flanken (stewed meat) and carrots cooked until they were falling-apart tender. Her homemade applesauce (made with the skins on so that it was slightly pink in color) was tart and sweet at the same time, and its finely strained texture was a treat to my tongue and a balm to my throat. The homemade sponge cake didn't have too much trouble going down either. When I was up to eating spaghetti and meatballs and spending most of my time either nagging her to entertain me, tormenting my brother, or making a mess of paper dolls in one room and paint and clay in the other, my mother pronounced me well enough to go to school.

I had run out of excuses. My temperature was normal, my throat had lost its swelling, and my aches and pains had vanished. My mother was desperate to get me out of the house—

probably to give her a chance to rest up before my brother came down with the mumps. The ice cube in my stomach, which had practically melted away from the heat of the mumps, came back as an icicle and pricked me every time I thought of facing the witch. She would have, in my absence, devised hundreds of ways to torture me for ruining her shoes. She would have turned the class against me. I could feel their sneers, their snickers hot on my back as I crawled back to my desk, flattened and defeated with humiliation and shame.

No amount of wailing and begging could put off the fateful day. My mother was resolute. The sick leave was over. As I headed off for school the next morning, dragging my feet through the slush, not even the thought that my mother had saved the last of the sponge cake for my lunch made the thought of facing that teacher and that classroom something I could tolerate. The closer I got, the slower I walked toward the ugly gray hulking mass of our elementary school, until some kids from my class raced past me, their boots spraying large icy drops of dirty snow onto their snow pants. One yelled back over his shoulder at me, ''Hey, did you know? We have a new teacher! She's young and really nice!'' They sped on leaving me stunned without waiting for a reply. I couldn't believe it. Someone had heard my prayers, although all I had modestly asked for was a one-day substitute, not a complete replacement. Like the sun breaking through the bleak overcast sky, a light came on somewhere in my chest, and the ice cube started to melt for good.

Split Pea Soup with Stewed Flanken

To my mind this is the quintessential midwinter belly warmer and spirit raiser.

1 pound split peas,
  well rinsed and drained
3 quarts beef or chicken stock
  or 3 quarts water and 3 beef
  or chicken bouillon cubes
  (I like Knorr's)
1½ pounds flanken (beef short
  ribs), available in kosher
  meat markets
1 large beef bone
1 large onion, sliced
3 cloves garlic, minced
2 teaspoons dried dill or
  ½ cup fresh dill
½ teaspoon dried oregano
1 bay leaf
3 stalks celery (including
  tops), sliced
4 carrots, peeled and sliced
Salt and freshly ground
  pepper, to taste

In a deep pot combine the peas, stock or water and bouillon, meat, beef bone, onion, garlic, and seasonings. Bring to a boil and skim the top. Lower the heat and simmer 1½ hours, uncovered.

Remove the bones and the flanken. Trim the meat and fat off the flanken and return the meat to the pot, discarding the bones and fat. Also discard the bay leaf. Add the celery and carrots to the soup and cook 1 more hour, adding water if the soup becomes too thick.

Cool slightly; remove the meat; puree the soup in a food processor, blender, or Foley food mill; season to taste with salt and freshly ground black pepper; and serve with chunks of meat.

Serves 8–10

Challa

½ cup warm water	¾ cup cold water
1 tablespoon sugar	3 extra large eggs plus 1 egg
2 tablespoons granulated yeast	white (reserve the yolk)
3 tablespoons vegetable oil	10 cups all-purpose flour,
1 tablespoon salt	approximately
3 tablespoons honey	2 tablespoons water
1 cup boiling water	¼ cup poppy or sesame seeds

Place the warm water and 1 tablespoon of sugar in a small bowl and sprinkle the yeast on top. Stir to dissolve. In a large bowl combine the oil, salt, honey, and boiling water. Add the cold water and stir until lukewarm. Add the yeast mixture. Beat the eggs and the egg white together and add them to the mixture. Stir in 4 cups of the flour; beat by hand or with an electric mixer fitted with a dough hook until well mixed. Add the remaining flour, a small amount at a time, until the dough is smooth, elastic, and no longer very sticky. Knead for an additional 10–15 minutes.

Place the dough in a large, oiled bowl and cover it with plastic wrap. Let it rise in a warm, draft-free place until it doubles in bulk. This will take about 1½–2 hours, depending on the temperature of the room. Punch the dough down and knead for 2 minutes. Divide in half. Cover 2 baking sheets with foil and lightly oil the foil.

Roll each part into a 12 × 14-inch rectangle and divide this lengthwise into 3 strips. Place the 3 ends together, pinching the dough to make them stay, and braid the strips. Repeat with the other half of the dough. Place the challas on the baking sheets and let them rise until doubled in size—about 45 minutes to 1 hour. Brush with the egg yolk beaten together with 2 tablespoons of water. Sprinkle generously with the poppy or sesame seeds.

While the loaves are rising, preheat the oven to 400 degrees with the rack in the center position. Place the loaves in the oven and immediately lower the oven temperature to 350. Bake for 35–45 minutes or until the loaves are golden brown and the bottoms sound hollow when lightly tapped. Cool the loaves on racks.

Makes 2 large challas

French Toast

2 tablespoons butter
1 whole egg
1 egg yolk
½ cup milk or light cream

1 tablespoon granulated sugar
1 teaspoon cinnamon
4 thick slices of challa or
   other egg bread

Melt the butter over low heat in a skillet or flat-bottomed sauté pan. Mix together the egg, egg yolk, milk or cream, sugar, and cinnamon. Dunk each slice of bread in the egg mixture long enough for some of the liquid to soak in. Use a spatula to transfer it to the pan. Cook until golden brown and then flip over to cook the other side, adding more butter if necessary. Serve with maple syrup.

Serves 2

Egg in the Nest

There is a great scene in the movie Moonstruck, *in which Olympia Dukakis, playing Cher's mother, makes her a breakfast consisting of slices of bread sautéed in olive oil. By the time she drops two eggs into the holes cut in the bread, the entire audience has transferred their lust for Nicholas Cage to the stuff cooking in that pan. Here is my version of that dish:*

2 thick (1-inch) and fairly wide slices of challa or any bread that has body but is still soft enough to make a hole in without falling apart	2 tablespoons butter 2 eggs Salt and pepper to taste

Use a 1½-inch round cookie cutter to cut a hole in the center of each piece of bread. Toast the challa. Melt the butter in a large frying pan and add the bread, turning once to coat both sides with butter. Drop an egg into each hole and cook over moderate heat until the eggs have just set up. You can try turning them once with a wide metal spatula if you prefer your eggs "over." Season with salt and pepper to taste.

Serves 1

Sweet-and-Sour Cabbage Soup

3 tablespoons vegetable oil
2 (1–1½ pounds) strips flanken (beef short ribs), available in kosher markets
2–3 quarts water
1 large can (16 ounces) tomatoes
2 onions, coarsely chopped
1 bay leaf
3 cloves garlic, minced
1 medium cabbage, shredded
4 tablespoons brown sugar
½ cup red wine vinegar
1 cup sauerkraut
Salt and pepper to taste

Heat the oil in the bottom of a 6-quart heavy-bottomed pot and sear the meat on both sides until it is browned. Drain off the fat and add the water, tomatoes, onions, and bay leaf. Bring to a simmer and skim the top. Reduce the heat, cover partially, and simmer for 1 hour. Remove the bay leaf. Add the garlic and cabbage and simmer another hour. Add the sugar, vinegar, and sauerkraut. Simmer an additional 15–20 minutes and then add salt and pepper to taste.

Serves 8

Lemon Sponge Cake

This "plain" cake is particularly good with a scoop of vanilla ice cream or served with the raspberry sauce found on page 93.

½ tablespoon solid vegetable
  shortening (such as Crisco)
6 extra large eggs at room
  temperature
1 cup sugar
2 tablespoons lemon juice
Finely grated rind of
  1 large lemon

1 cup cake flour, measured
  after sifting
¼ teaspoon salt, sifted with
  the flour
¼ teaspoon salt
Confectioners sugar

Preheat the oven to 325 degrees with the rack in the lower third, but not the lowest, position. Use the shortening to grease the bottom (but not the sides) of a 10-inch tube pan with a removeable bottom. Cut a piece of parchment to fit the bottom, fit it in place, and lightly grease it and then dust it with flour.

Place the eggs and sugar in the bowl of an electric mixer and beat at high speed for about 10–15 minutes or until the mixture is very thick and forms a heavy, light yellow ribbon when the beaters are lifted from the bowl. Add the lemon juice and rind and continue mixing for 3 more minutes. Remove the bowl from the mixer.

Sift half the salt/flour mixture at 1 time over the egg/sugar mixture and fold in gently, using a rubber spatula. Repeat with the rest of the flour. Make sure no traces of flour remain, being careful not to overwork the batter. Pour the batter into the prepared pan, smoothing the top with the rubber spatula. Bake 50 minutes or until a cake tester or toothpick inserted in the center comes out clean.

Invert the cake pan on top of a rack to cool. If the pan comes with little feet, just invert it on a counter. When the cake has cooled to room temperature, remove the pan, invert the cake onto a flat plate, and sift some confectioners sugar on it.

Serves 8–10

The Toni Girl

In seventh grade if you were a girl with straight hair your life was ruined. No self-respecting preteen worth her salt would show up at school with stick-straight hair; even moderately wavy hair wouldn't do. If you didn't have a poodle cut, you might as well just turn in your training bra, burn your gum wrapper chains, and forget about having anyone of the opposite sex join you in a round of Five Minutes in the Closet with the Lights Off (the game that came after everyone got bored with Spin the Bottle). My hair was so straight that slicking on a whole jar of Jokur (the ancestor of mousse), looping it tightly around my finger in a pin curl, and anchoring it with three bobby pins for a night would only produce sores on my scalp and pieces of rigid mousey wisps and sprays that stuck out at strange angles from my head. Toni Home Permanent changed all that. Now any girl could have curls, went the advertisement, and one long session with my mother's friend Flo turned my ordinary wimpy strands into something a pad of Brillo would envy.

Flo lived in a brick housing project somewhere in Hartford. She was my mother's Italian friend (although for years I thought she was a Jew who spoke with an Italian accent) who had once attended beauty school and did her girlfriends favors by giving them and their daughters home permanents.

Getting a permanent from Flo was always a good news, bad news affair. The process was so painful and smelled so bad that my eyes would be red and swollen from tears of pain and irritation from the chemicals. Worse, the immediate results were horrifying—the new curls were so tight and springy that all you had to do was add some cleaner and I could have used my head as a soap pad. The final insult was that the chemical smell lingered (you couldn't wash your hair for two days after the perm) so everyone knew what you had been up to and signaled it by grimacing with repulsion and rapidly waving their hands in front of their noses. The twofold good news was that after the perm settled down, I had a mop of natural-looking curls for the next six months, and Flo made the best tomato sauce in the whole world.

A trip to Flo's was, pain and suffering aside, an experience I looked forward to. The door opened and out roared the wonderful smell of foods Italian—garlic, onions cooked in olive oil, the famous tomato sauce simmering in the big black kettle on the back of the stove. The powerful aroma of that night's dinner hit my head like an express train—the combination of onions, pepper, and potatoes hung suspended in the doorway like a heavily cluttered charm bracelet. Then there was the noise, the TV and the radio going full blast so that a low melodious voice droned on about the soothing, refreshing brace of Aqua Velva while a peppy, harmonious singing group advised us to "Get sharp, to feel sharp—with Gillette." This base noise was jarringly overridden by the astonishing racket of several dozen birds, in cages, everywhere around the place. Flocks of canaries that chirped and flashed like caution lights, back and forth, back and forth in their cages, pearly gray and ruby-headed lovebirds that cooed and necked, phosphorescent parakeets bobbing and pecking at each other, and a nasty parrot that imitated the sound of the telephone perfectly and then called, "I'll get it!" His only other phrase was "Tie 'er up, Flo, tie 'er up," which he screamed over and over as Flo festooned my aching scalp with the tiny pink curlers.

The top layer of noise was Flo. Flo with a butt set in the corner of her bright red mouth, laughing and talking nonstop in a thick accent that was a Bronx/Naples combo. Like a pizza with hot dogs on it. Her favorite phrase, which she pronounced at least a hundred times while the tears streamed down my face and my nose ran into my collar, was "Hey honey, I toldja it hoits to be-a beautiful." Flo looked like a Betty Grable pinup wrapped up in a cobbler's apron, except for her hair—you never knew which style and color it would be from one week to the next. Her hands were perfectly manicured and her long, filed nails were painted with exotic colors with names like Burnished Copper and Heart on Fire Red.

I loved being one of the girls while Mom and Flo smoked a Pall Mall, drank a cup of Maxwell House, and gossiped about who was having early menopause, giggled over jokes I didn't get (but pretended to), and fixed each other's hair in wild styles they never would have worn out the door. Flo kept trying to convince my mother to try a new color like her own unearthly red, but my mother wisely demurred.

Alice and Ralph Kramden argued in the background or Ricky warned Lucy that she had some "splainin to do," I got to cover the birds to stop their racket, and then it was time to get down to work. I sat on two phone books perched on a vinyl-covered chair next to the kitchen table. Flo draped an old shower curtain around my shoulders and pinned it shut with a long metal hair clip. Starting at the nape of my neck she tugged and wound tiny sections of hair around little pink curlers, then looped the elastic ends of the rods around to secure them in place, every once in a while firmly pushing down on the top of my head so that my chin dug into my upper chest. Meanwhile my scalp felt like it was being separated from my skull. My eyes ached, straining upward for distraction from the agony above them, but all I could see was the cage of the nasty parrot, balanced on two baby-blue-painted cinder blocks in the corner. He tugged and pulled at his gingham cage cover until it slid off and he began his raucous cry: "Tie 'er up, Flo, tie 'er up."

"Shuddup-a you goddamn boid!" roared Flo, scattering cigarette ashes into the curler tray. The bird rolled its black beady eyes and chewed on its foot for a while, gathering strength to do its phone imitation. At the point when my neck felt stretched out like a cartoon character's, Flo would snap my head back and start on the front. Soon neat rows of pink blossomed where once there was normal brown hair; I had a head full of plastic corn-rows. Next Flo took a small plastic squeeze bottle full of vile-smelling liquid and squirted a generous amount across each rod. The stuff trickled onto my scalp and stung like the dickens. She anchored me to the chair with her hand firmly on my shoulder yelling, "Sit still, you-a know it hoits to be-a beautiful." The solution dripped down my scalp and down my neck into the towel tucked into the top of the shower curtain. Of course my nose reacted by first itching like crazy and then running. My hands, trapped inside the curtain, were twitching to get out and rub my face. There were more yells of "SIT STILL!!!" from Flo and "TIE 'ER UP!!!" from the boid. I was a prisoner of beauty—where the hell was my prince?

When finally Flo decided that the curl had "taken," it was time for the neutralizer, which was applied while I leaned over and my mother held my head (face down) over Flo's kitchen sink. The final step was to rinse off the solutions under the faucet. Flo briskly dried my head with a big towel—since the rods were still in place this was additional torture. Finally I was returned to the kitchen chair where the two women whipped out the pink curlers and exclaimed over the results.

In the darkened kitchen window I could make out my new reflection; as much as I had steeled myself for the shock my heart always sunk to my knees when I saw the orderly rows of cork-screws springing energetically up around my thin face—this was not something found in nature. Together with my swollen eyes and red nose I looked like a preteen Martian (not to mention that I smelled like a chemical plant on fire). But my mother and Flo were somehow always overjoyed with the results and Flo, as if reading my mind, always assured me that in two days the smell would be gone and the curls would calm down so that I would look quite normal.

My mother cleaned up the debris from the perm, and Flo put on another pot of Maxwell House and boiled up a large pot of water to cook some pasta. On the kitchen table soon appeared a steaming bowl of spaghetti topped with the famous red sauce, a tray of cannoli, and a gorgeous cheese pie. As Flo dished out the pasta, I watched her long ruby nails flash and sighed, wondering if my father would change his mind about nail polish.

"Mario! Kids!! Come and eat!" In the back room Flo's husband and her two sons turned off the ball game and came to the table. The boys' eyes widened with amazement as they took in my transformation. Fortunately they had the good manners not to giggle. Mario ruffled my curls (I tried not to wince) and pronounced me "gee-orgeous."

I viewed that plate of pasta and those cannoli as my Holy Grail; what agony I had to endure to get to enjoy them, and what a just reward they were. The red sauce tasted as heavenly rich as it smelled, and the cannoli—the shells were so delicate and tender that when you lifted one to your mouth you automatically cupped the other hand underneath to catch the fallout of pieces of shell and confectioners sugar. The filling was Flo's pride and joy, made with something she pronounced "ri-gut." It took me years to figure out that she was saying ricotta. It was vaguely sweet but never cloying, with slivers of orange peel and a hint of rum. My mother let me have a half a cup of coffee (cut with a lot of milk) to complete the treat. The cheese pie was a masterpiece, made with more ri-gut, golden raisins, and toasted pine nuts on top. We always got to take a few generous slices home along with a jar of Flo's famous tomato sauce.

That night in bed, fingering the miniature shock absorbers that made up my new and unfamiliar hairdo, I reflected a bit on the important things in life. I knew that no matter how much pain I was willing to subject myself to, I would never be beautiful (although I was convinced that long spiky nails with red polish would certainly help. . .); making a good cannoli and cheese pie from scratch would probably, in the long run, make up for stick-straight hair. I sure hoped so.

Tomato Sauce

1 tablespoon olive oil
1 medium onion,
  coarsely chopped
2 cloves garlic, minced
1 28-ounce can whole, peeled
  tomatoes

1 small (6-ounce) can
  tomato paste
¾ cup water
1 teaspoon sugar
1 teaspoon dried oregano
1 teaspoon dried basil
Salt and pepper to taste

Heat the olive oil in a sauté pan and cook the onion until it is transparent. Add the garlic and cook briefly over low heat for about 1 minute, taking care not to burn the garlic. Add the tomatoes in their liquid, the tomato paste, and water. Mash the tomatoes with a wooden spoon and stir. Add the sugar and spices and then finally the salt and pepper to taste. Cover and cook on very low heat for 2 hours. Add additional basil and oregano to taste.

Makes about 1 quart

Cheese Pie

FOR THE CRUST

2 cups flour, measured after
   sifting
1½ sticks (6 ounces) sweet
   (unsalted) butter, cold, cut
   into pieces

4 extra large egg yolks
¼ cup sugar
Finely grated peel of 1 lemon
Pinch of salt

Place all the ingredients in the work bowl of an electric mixer or food processor fitted with the metal blade. Mix on medium speed or process with an on-and-off motion until the dough forms a ball. Break off about ¼ of the dough and then form both portions into balls. Flatten the balls, wrap them in plastic, and refrigerate for ½ hour.

Butter a 9 × 1½-inch springform pan and then dust it with flour. Roll ¾ of the dough out into an 11-inch circle on a lightly floured board. Fit the dough into the prepared pan and press it into the bottom and up the sides, trimming away any excess. Roll out the remaining dough into a rectangle about 12 inches long, and cut this dough into ½-inch wide strips.

FOR THE FILLING AND ASSEMBLY

⅓ cup brandy
⅓ cup golden raisins
2½ pounds (approximately
   5 cups) whole milk ricotta
⅔ cup sugar
1½ teaspoons almond extract

Finely grated rind of 1 lemon
4 extra large egg yolks
⅓ cup toasted pine nuts
   (see note below)
1 egg white and 1 tablespoon
   water lightly beaten together

Preheat the oven to 350 degrees with the rack in the center position. Heat the brandy in a small saucepan and add the raisins. Cook for 1 minute over moderate heat, stirring or shaking the pan constantly. Set aside while you prepare the rest of the filling. In the work bowl of an electric mixer, or by hand, beat the ricotta with the sugar, almond extract, and lemon rind. When it is smooth, beat in the egg yolks, one at a time, taking care to make sure they are completely incorporated. Stir in the raisins and brandy.

Pour the filling into the prepared pan and use a rubber scraper to smooth the top. Sprinkle the toasted pine nuts on top. Place the pastry strips across the top of the pie in a crisscross design, trimming off the excess ends. Brush the strips with the egg wash. Bake for 1 hour and 10 minutes or until the crust is lightly brown and the filling is set and feels firm to the touch.

Remove the pie from the oven and let it set for 5 minutes. Remove the springform sides (you may have to run a small sharp knife around the inside edge to release it) and finish cooling at room temperature. Serve at room temperature or chilled.

Serves 10

NOTE: TO TOAST PINE NUTS

Heat 2 tablespoons of vegetable oil in a skillet. When the oil is hot add the pine nuts and shake the pan gently back and forth over moderate heat, moving the nuts back and forth in the oil. When the nuts are golden brown remove them to paper towels to drain.

Cannoli

While homemade cannoli shells are hard to beat, they do take some time and patience to make. A perfectly sensible alternative is to buy some from your favorite Italian bakery and fill them with homemade filling. These cannoli shells can be made weeks in advance and stored in a cool dry place.

FOR THE CANNOLI SHELLS

3 cups flour, measured after sifting
3 tablespoons sweet (unsalted) butter, melted
1½ tablespoons sugar

¾ cup (approximately) sweet marsala
Pinch of salt
White of 1 egg beaten with ½ teaspoon water
Corn oil for frying

Combine the flour, butter, sugar, salt, and mix well. Dribble in enough wine to make a stiff but movable dough. Turn out onto a lightly floured board and knead for 10–15 minutes or until the dough is smooth and soft, adding more flour if necessary to keep the dough from sticking. Form the dough into a ball, cover with plastic wrap, and refrigerate for 1 hour.

Divide the dough in half, and working with ½ at a time roll the dough out as thin as possible on a floured board. Using a floured biscuit cutter or glass, cut the dough into 4-inch circles. Wrap each circle around a cannoli tube, overlapping the edges slightly, moisten them with the beaten egg white, and press together to seal the seam.

Using a deep frying pan or skillet, pour oil to a depth of 3 inches. Using a deep frying thermometer to test, heat the oil to 375 degrees. Fry the cannoli, 2 or 3 at a time, until they are a deep, golden brown. Use tongs to turn them over so they cook uniformly. Drain on several layers of paper towels. Cool completely before carefully removing the metal forms.

FOR THE RICOTTA FILLING

3 pounds whole milk ricotta
¾ cup confectioners sugar
¼–⅓ cup Grand Marnier or
    other liqueur of your choice

Finely grated rind of 2
    brightly colored oranges
⅓ cup tiny chocolate chips
    (optional)

Place the ricotta in the bowl of an electric mixer and mix on medium speed for about 3 minutes or until the cheese is very smooth. On low speed add the sugar, liqueur, and orange peel. Beat another 2 minutes at moderate speed. On low speed mix in the chocolate chips.

TO ASSEMBLE

Confectioners sugar

It is best to fill the cannoli just before you plan to eat them. Fill a pastry bag fitted with a large, wide (number 9) tube with the filling. Press filling into each end of the shell, forcing it toward the middle and letting some show on either end. Dust with confectioners sugar.

Makes about 2 dozen

Chips

It took me years to be able to come to terms with the fact that my grandmother was crazy.

When people say, "Oy, did I come from a crazy family," I think, they don't know from crazy. My grandmother was Crazy. Somehow, ever since the total acceptance, in fact the passionate embrace, of the culture of neurosis, the crazier your family, the higher your status among your peers. While the craziness of your family isn't quite the first thing you talk about to new acquaintances, as soon as you've finished talking about how much (or how little) you paid for your house, your lawn service, your kid's Suzuki lessons, and what's wrong (right) with the local schools, local government, how you haven't started saving for college but plan to right after this upcoming trip to Club Med, where you grew up, went to school, who you know, etc., etc., doesn't it always somehow come around to families—and how crazy yours was?

Good crazy-family stories are best passed around at small dinner parties where the guests don't know each other well and need a topic in common to get things rolling. Orphans aside, we all have families and they are all crazy. Come on, haven't you sat around a clunky, oversized, dark-stained oak coffee table (the kind with claw feet that used to be a library table when people still had libraries, before it was cut down for a coffee table) sipping dark beer and pigging out on Doritos and salsa, making everyone else scream with laughter about how your mother on her way to visit a friend in the city got into the elevator which instead of heading up to 15G went down into the subbasement. When the doors opened, in strolled an unsavory looking character in a black leather jacket with a large Doberman pinscher. As the elevator doors closed the man yelled, "Sit!" and your mother promptly sat on the floor. Hah, hah, hah, hah. Much laughter at your poor mother's expense. How about the one about Uncle Abe, oldest resident of the Hebrew Home, who got into a fistfight with his roommate over which of them had the longer Haftorah at their Bar Mitzvah seventy-seven years ago in a Brooklyn shul no longer in existence. All you children (without high blood pressure, incontinence, cataracts, and false teeth) laughing at your families' craziness. I am here to tell you that this is not crazy; confused, maybe; insecure, perhaps; endearingly and amusingly eccentric—most likely.

Hearing about the craziness of my maternal grandmother will most likely cause you to ease up on your families.

My grandmother was certifiably nuts and my grandfather was nuts by proxy. Delusions of grandeur do not begin to explain the ends to which my grandmother went to establish and maintain her sovereignty in the kingdom of her third-floor walk-up. Her dutiful subjects (her children, their children, and the children of her childrens' children) had to address her as "Mater," an affectation held over from her Liverpool days where she spent her youth. She was a short, round, dimpled bleached-blond monarch in pink curlers, and it's said she had been a beauty in her youth. Blind as a bat, she refused to wear glasses lest she become dependent on them, so every encounter with her was, by necessity, nose to nose. I remember her as sort of a working-class Helena Rubinstein.

She had beautiful skin always carefully made up and dusted with flesh-colored powder, her plump arms felt like down pillows covered with the smoothest, softest satin, and her cheeks painstakingly painted with two bright circles of rouge, remained smooth and unlined well into her eighties. I don't think I ever saw her without lipstick, even though her crown of hair curlers were never set free of their peroxided strands. Her small, sharp, yellow-brown round eyes were miscast in her face; they were the first warning that you should not be misled by her softly dimpled exterior. She may have looked like a tidy Austrian featherbed, but make no mistake, her filling was really horsehair and steel filings. My mother once told me that my grandfather (the mildest and most gentle of human beings) was driven to bouts of frenzied jealousy by her beauty. So sure was he that she was taking lovers while he was at work, he would occasionally sneak back into the house and hide in the closet waiting for her to show her true stuff. She, on the other hand, blissfully unaware (or, on second thought, perhaps very aware) of his secret scrutiny, would do her housework while bellowing out a ditty about a woman who married a man who had no hips at all.

While my grandfather (a tailor by trade) pumped away at his treadle Singer, tape measures hanging around his neck and common pins pressed firmly between his lips, my grandmother made a career out of writing letters to the editor. Multipaged, handwritten diatribes were daily dashed off to the editor of the two Hartford papers, to the Jewish dailies, to women's magazines, to radio stations. My grandmother's mighty pen spewed out her violent reaction to topics from the pope's snubbing of Golda Meir to a rise in the price of cauliflower. She wrote to her congressman, her senator, and to presidents from Calvin Coolidge to Gerald Ford. She publicized her opinions about nature, love, family, and civic responsibility in speeches that she would give at the drop of a hat at any gathering of any kind and of any size. Before every wedding and Bar Mitzvah, one of the most important details was to negotiate with Mater about the length and topic of her speech. There was never any debate about the fact that there would be a speech, and there was certainly only the fantasy of control after having broached the issue with her. Truth was, you never knew what the hell she would get up and start expostulating about. One thing was for certain, she would cover (and with great emotion) all of her favorite topics from America: Land of Opportunity, to her life story (which to me seemed sort of backwards; after all, wasn't she some kind of poor but titled royalty in England and here in Hartford she was just another, if slightly off her rocker, character—a true rags-to-shmate saga).

She wrote schmaltzy poetry in which the last word of each line rhymed with the previous and following line—even if it made no sense whatsoever. She always seemed to speak in the lecture mode, perched on her invisible soapbox, wagging her finger and snapping her eyes. Her curlers would bob around in their yellow moorings while the red lips would carefully enunciate, in a studied upper-class British accent, outrageous and flagrantly bizarre thoughts.

She had absolutely no idea how to relate to her grandchildren. I guess she had given it her all when it came to her own children and simply taken an early retirement when they grew up. She made up strange and terrifying stories to scare us kids from eating trayf (nonkosher food) and mixing dairy and meat dishes—cold milk would turn the fat in the meat into a rock-hard glob in your stomach and it would stay there forever in your body eternally gumming up the works; eating even the smallest bite of lobster would result in a horrible and agonizingly prolonged death and no rabbi would preside at your funeral because you died of eating trayf. Every chance she got she would pinch my nose painfully hard to make it small, and she insisted that I sleep with a button pressed into my cheek to give me a dimple. Clearly this was not a granny from central casting who would haul you up on her lap for a few nursery rhymes or choruses of ''The Farmer in the Dell.''

Some of the things she told me scared me silly, but mostly I had the sense not to pay her much attention, although I was careful to duck when she grabbed for my nose, and I didn't eat lobster until I was an adult.

Are you wondering if she could cook? After all, this is a book about food, and all I've done so far is talk about how my grandmother and I were not a match made in heaven. Well, in fact, she couldn't cook at all—with one major exception: she made the world's best French fried potatoes—which she called, simply ''chips.'' The secret of the chips was that they were cooked in something my grandmother called sweet oil and chicken fat.

My grandfather, defying every study ever issued by the American Heart Association, lived ninety-eight years on a diet of chicken fat. While his eyes and ears failed him at the end, his heart was strong and healthy and his arteries operated at full capacity up to the last days of his life. My grandmother was not trying to disprove the statistics; it was that she simply cooked everything in chicken fat, aka, Jewish Crisco. The only dish that was worth risking life and arteries over were her chips. This dish was the only reason that I could be persuaded to visit her.

I had to start nagging about the chips the minute I walked into her house because she hated to cook and had many good excuses not to: too hot, too much work for one person eating, I don't have any potatoes, frying makes a mess, it smells up the house (I thought the house always smelled like she had just finished frying something in chicken fat), you'll ruin your lunch (dinner), etc., etc. The only way to get her to budge (along with several minutes of prime whining—I would never stoop to compliments) was to offer to dust the thousands of chachkes in the parlor. At that point she sometimes (but very grudgingly) relented but not before shooting me the classic you-don't-deserve-this-you-spoiled-child look. So, I took up the dust cloth and she would rather imperiously don her apron and rummage around assembling the onions, potatoes, and the jar of chicken fat from the refrigerator.

The cast-iron skillet that she used was housed permanently on the top of the stove. It weighed a ton and was seriously encrusted from decades of use without ever being washed but simply wiped out when she was finished cooking. Into the pan went a healthy two inches of something she called sweet oil and a scoop of solid, yellow chicken fat—enough to clog the arteries of every Jewish man on the eastern seaboard. As the gas flame licked the bottom and sides of the pan, liquifying the fat, Mater turned her attention to the onions.

Mater cooked like a sailor, slamming onions down on the drain board as if to subdue them before the final torture of frying in deep fat. She used her all-purpose (and only) knife to peel them informally (who cared if some of the outer skin stayed on) and hack them into random sizes. She scooped up the pieces with her hands and Plop! Sizzle! into the pan they tumbled, making a loud, protesting noise as the fat sprayed in painful splatters on those who dared stand too close. Mater peeled the potatoes with the same lackadaisical effort that she did the onions; consequently large pieces of peel and an occasional nubby eye were part of the chips' physiognomy. Like the onions, the potatoes were hacked into thick, uneven chunks. Now, the next steps were the secret of the chips' deliciousness: Mater dried each raw slice very carefully with a dish towel, removing as much surface moisture as possible, and then she waited until the onions were fried to a very deep brown before she added the potatoes, a few slices at a time, to the pan.

The smell wafting out into the parlour made me delirious with desire. The heady scent of onions frying was the Chanel No. 5 of my formative years. As I unenergetically waved the dust cloth

over the bowl of wax fruit on the marble-topped mahogany coffee table, I glanced to see if I could find the dent in the apple
that was left there by my brother one Sunday morning when out
of boredom and hunger he took a bite. Dusting the heavy china
figurines, I rearranged their groupings so that the snooty Vic-
torian lady with the parasol and the little white dog jumping
at her heels was now being chased by a Huck Finn sort of
character with bare feet and a fishing pole. Mater's extensive collection of intricately carved ivory miniatures was more of a
challenge to clean. I would marvel at the thought of someone
actually fashioning something so tiny and so perfect as that three-
inch hunched-over Chinaman straining to pull a rickshaw and
the five-tiered pagoda whose every surface was embellished with
cutouts and curlicues. Four shelves of faux Degas ballerinas,
shepherds and their frozen flocks, dancing poodles made from
pink blown glass, a family of bluebirds that refused to stay
upright, and a grouping of assorted horses (one of which had
a broken leg that was splinted with half a toothpick and some
Elmer's glue). I stuck a tiny blue teapot under the horse's nose
so that he could take a drink when no one was looking.

The scraping noise of Mater's moving the heavy iron pan back
and forth on the burner brought me back to reality. The aroma
was unbearably enticing—if the smell of French fries cooking at
a fast-food place is all you have to go by, believe me, the two
smells are not even in the same ballpark.

My last (and least favorite) job was the two bonsai plants. Not
only were they hard to dust, and smelled peculiar, they just plain
gave me the creeps. Here was this weird-looking, shrunken,
twisted tree anchored in a milky green ceramic bowl with a thick,
featureless ceramic statue of what was supposed to be a wise
Chinese guy standing under it. This bonsai tree was (according
to Mater's admonitions not to in any way harm this priceless
thing) supposed to be a thousand years old and worth a fortune.
She watered it once a month, myopically holding an eyedropper
over the minute gnarled limbs with such reverential love and
devotion that it made me want to damage the thing so that it
would die—although to me it already looked dead, how would
she ever know the difference? I settled for taking a swipe with
my finger around the figurine's coolie hat, blowing the obvious
dust off the sides of the bowl, and then I called it a day.

In the kitchen Mater had dumped the cooked chips onto a ripped-open brown paper sack to blot off some of the grease. Then she sprinkled them with a little vinegar and lots of salt and pepper, ladling them onto a plate that she then set upon the oilcloth-covered kitchen table. Next she poured the fat from the pan back into a can for anything else that might need frying, wiped out the pan with more brown paper, placed her hands on her hips, and fixed her small yellow eyes on me. "What do you say?" she asked, sticking her face close to mine so I could see the beads of sweat gathered on her brow, ready to roll down leaving red tracks through her rouged cheeks. I noticed her mustache was the same color as her curls.

"Thank you, Mater," I replied with one of those phoney put-on angelic smiles that I know she saw right through—the kind of smile that could have gone hand in hand with a wiseass curt-sy if I hadn't already been sitting down.

I can remember like it was yesterday, sitting on that wooden kitchen chair, the vinyl sticking to my skin, my legs swinging in anticipation as I waited for the chips to cool down so I could eat them without scalding the inside of my mouth. Cheeks on fists, I leaned low over the plate so that the aroma enveloped my face. The first things that I went for were the blackened pieces of onion, crisp and bitter and laden with crystals of salt. Then the chips, the browned outsides crackly and hard and the insides white, fluffy, soft, and steaming hot. These were not one bite affairs but three or four mouthfuls of heaven served up in each chip.

I ate them with my fingers, taking carefully slow, thoughtful bites, surreptitiously wiping away the grease on my shorts, or T-shirt, occasionally pausing to lick the salt and oil from my hands and mouth. This fifty-pound weakling could pack away as much as Mater had made and in short order. I remember feeling guilty for the many times I wished I could trade this unconventionally difficult and certainly crazy grandmother for a more traditional, predictable one, except right after she had made me chips—then she wasn't really so bad.

Chips

4–5 large Idaho potatoes, peeled
2 large onions
1 cup (approximately)
vegetable oil

3 tablespoons rendered
chicken fat (optional), see
note below
Salt and freshly ground black
pepper to taste
White vinegar

Cut the potatoes into 1-inch slices and use paper towels to very thoroughly press as much moisture as possible from the slices. Slice the onion into ½-inch thick rounds. Heat ½ cup of the oil and the optional chicken fat, and 2 tablespoons of the optional chicken fat in a large cast-iron skillet.

When the oil is hot, add half the onions and cook until they are dark brown, but not burnt. (If you like the onions very dark and crisp leave them in the pan when you add the potatoes. If not, remove them at this point with a slotted spoon, drain them on paper towels, and combine them with the potatoes after cooking.) Repeat with the other onions. Add more oil, if necessary, and when it is hot place some of the potatoes in the pan, taking care not to crowd them, lower the heat to moderate, and cook for about 20 minutes, then turn the slices over and repeat on the other side. If the potatoes are browning too fast, lower the heat. It is important for them to both brown and be cooked inside—you can test for doneness with a fork. As the potatoes are ready, place them on paper towels to drain. Combine the onions and potatoes, sprinkle liberally with salt and pepper and a few drops of vinegar.

Serves 4

NOTE: TO RENDER CHICKEN FAT

This is the fat that has been melted off the chicken during the cooking process. The easiest way to get chicken fat is to skim it off the top of homemade chicken soup—actually, the really easiest way is to buy chicken fat from the kosher market (the small jars can be kept in the freezer forever). Lacking a kosher meat market and/or chicken soup, the next easiest way is to pull off some of the fat that surrounds the bottom cavity of a fresh chicken. Place the fat in a small frying pan set over moderate heat and cook, moving the fat back and forth, until the fat melts and you are left with several tablespoons of golden liquid. Strain and store in the freezer until needed.

Thanksgiving

The fall that our eldest son was in third grade we took him to visit Plimoth Plantation. As we sat in a darkened auditorium watching a film about the voyage of the *Mayflower*, I saw him carefully scrutinizing a facsimile of the ship's manifest. He was looking for his family name among the Adamses and Winthrops.

Later during the tour he observed with the same steady intensity a group of simulated Pilgrims solemnly and with great civility and formality enjoying a mock Thanksgiving feast with several unsmiling and intimidatingly stern Indians in full dress. The rough wooden table was set with pewter porringers and wooden trenchers that were shared between the diners. The only utensils were pewter spoons, which were also shared. Before the meal the family and guests clasped hands in prayer and then quietly began the pleasant business of putting away the simple but delicious-looking bounty served to them by the older children. It was a moving reminder, watching the Pilgrims in their homespun clothing and the native Americans in their feathers and skins, of what the first Thanksgivings might have been like.

Our son was very quiet on the ride home, and it wasn't until I tucked him into bed that night that he could articulate what was troubling him. "Mommy," he asked, "which is the real Thanksgiving, ours or theirs?

I knew just what he was talking about. There certainly wasn't a whole lot of similarity between the way those Pilgrims were celebrating their Thanksgiving and the way our family did. The difference was about as far apart as Plymouth, Massachusetts, is from Ellis Island, New York.

My first eight Thanksgivings were celebrated at my aunt's house on Magnolia Street in Hartford, Connecticut. The heavy, rectangular mahogany dining room table and its sidekick, the mahogany lowboy, took up almost all the floor space in the room so that squeezing the fifteen or so chairs needed to seat our family was a logistical endeavor that took my Uncle Herman all of two days to figure out. Somehow (to my embarrassment and fury) I always got stuck sitting on the stool that usually lived next to the telephone table. It took two volumes of yellow pages to bring me up to chest level with the table. The table was set with a white damask cloth covered with faded and barely discernible mementos of past Thanksgivings (the faint blue splotch where my mother had dropped a juicy piece of blueberry pie destined for my Aunt Rose's plate; the once brown, now grayish streak where my brother and I had fought over a glass of cream soda. I won—the rest of the streak ruined his new white shirt; assorted cranberry sauce and gravy markings of Thanksgivings gone by). My job was to help set the table.

As I distributed the neat stack of carefuly folded damask napkins around the table, I pictured my mother sitting at the big white ironing machine, perspiration gleaming on her face as she worked the foot pedals and manipulated the crumpled damp squares of fabric through the giant rollers. Out they would come from the back side of the machine, flat as pancakes and smooth as a fresh piece of paper. I carefully untied the ribbons holding the cloth rolls and slipped the heavy silver forks, spoons, and knives from their felt-lined sleeves and placed them in a triangle around each napkin. Standing back to admire my creative treatment I knew that soon a grown-up would come by and tell me that I was wasting time and getting my fingerprints all over the silver they had just worked so hard to polish. Grown-ups simply had no imagination.

The center of the table held a turkey/pumpkin/Pilgrim motif made, usually by me, out of bits and pieces of construction paper (cut with those lousy scissors they give little kids so they won't hurt themselves and are so dull they are incapable of cutting anything), accumulated chestnuts, acorns, pipe cleaners, and popsicle sticks. Larged dried gobs of Elmer's glue and designs drawn with stubs of fat brown and orange Crayola crayons completed the effort. One year I made Pilgrim collars for everyone to wear. My Aunt Rose was the only one who was a good enough sport to wear it but accidentally set hers on fire as she was making the gravy for the turkey.

Strange as it may seem, the strongest memory I have of what went on at that table (besides the food, of course) was the plates themselves. Now, here's what really set us apart from the Pilgrims and their ancestors: one of my aunts had, very early on, discovered an alternative to china dishes—plastic dishes. They were, I believe, called Melamite. Back in the early fifties when most of the objects that people cooked with or ate off of were made out of "real" materials—wood, metal, glass, etc.—these dull, off-white, lifeless dishes caused a minor revolution. They never broke. They never chipped and they never cracked. You could throw them on the table, in the sink, at your husband or your kids without every worrying about having to replace them. I remember the first Thanksgiving they appeared. My aunt had really gone to town—bought them in every size and shape they came in. They were the most alien thing I had ever seen—and weird to eat off of as well. As soon as you managed to skewer something on your fork, it took to sliding around on the slick surface of the plate so it was impossible to get the right leverage to attack it with your knife. Consequently, bits and pieces of food skittered right off the edges of your plate and were relegated to the netherworld beneath the rims where they sat throughout the meal, making new landmarks of their own on the tablecloth. These dishes ultimately became their own curse—they never did break, they just got gray and grungy looking and stuck around for years. We tried everything from melting them to dropping them out of the attic window, but like the proverbial cat, they always came back. I think to this day my aunt (the enthusiastic purchaser) uses them under potted plants.

Well, the Pilgrims had their pewter and we had our plastic. The differences didn't stop there. Their calm was our chaos. The rule of thumb was that all the men and the kids got to sit throughout the meal. All the women got to jump up and down, run back and forth into the kitchen ferrying large steaming platters of food one way and empty dishes on the return trip, meanwhile urging all those seated to eat more and all the other running mothers, grandmothers, and aunts to "sit down, for God's sake." Grand Central Station at rush hour couldn't have had more traffic.

Our Thanksgiving menu had less to do with the fall bounty than it had to do with the fact that on Magnolia Street every one of our family gatherings that involved food (and they *all* involved food) had almost the same menu. Only the main course changed. Every meal started off with matzo ball soup. Thanksgiving, Rosh Hashanah—no difference. Next, chopped liver with onion slices. Then depending on the whim of the cook we had either roast beef (cooked to within an inch of this side of burnt) or turkey. In the case of Thanksgiving we always had turkey. In the potato department our serving dishes ranneth over. We had roast potatoes, mashed potatoes, and my mother's special candied sweet potatoes, made with orange juice, Grand Marnier, and brown sugar. Green vegetables were not considered an important part of the event so they usually languished, in the form of overcooked green beans, cooled and unloved in one of those plastic dishes in the center of the table partially obscured by the centerpiece. Desserts took the form of pie—apple and blueberry—made by my mother, who raised pie-making to a new art form. We ate until we could barely move, reminding ourselves that, after all, this was Thanksgiving and one was expected to eat to full potential.

After dinner the grown-ups sat around drinking coffee and smoking cigarettes. The kids drifted upstairs to play spit (a raucous card game that involves trying to maim your opponent—or at least that's what my cousins told me the rules were every time they smashed my hand) or hide in the closet to smoke purloined Lucky Strikes. When we started to fight, it was time to go home.

As an adult I made a few misguided attempts to establish my own Thanksgiving traditions. I served fancy canapés made out of foods no one could pronounce and that the kids thought tasted disgusting. I served insipid trendy cocktails concocted from fruit juices, white wine, and mulling spices when my parents really wanted a scotch on the rocks. The china and silver accumulated as wedding gifts made a rare appearance on our glass and chrome table. No plastic dishes ever graced our hand-embroidered Portuguese place mats—the ones that were cheaper to buy than to dry clean. Elaborate fall flower arrangements graced the center of the table and made it impossible for people to see each other. I scoured cookbooks for international Thanksgiving menu ideas and that's how, one year, we started our meal with cold cherry soup on the coldest day of November. With total disregard for what my family was accustomed to (never mind liked), I foisted on them an obnoxious assortment of faux Thanksgiving dishes from pumpkin fritters to boned stuffed turkey roulade. I cut back on the butter and offered four different kinds of vegetables cooked only seconds beyond raw. To add insult to injury, I hired a maid to serve and wash the dishes.

When my parents made noises about going to Florida early and my kids suggested that they had friends who had normal homes where they might run away to for this holiday, I saw the light. And while I didn't run out and buy Melamite dishes, I did manage to dig out that old damask cloth with the stains of Thanksgivings past, and I do make matzo ball soup, chopped liver, and three kinds of potatoes. Chaos is making a comeback but no one smokes (to my knowledge). The kids play spit, and while this maybe isn't exactly what the Pilgrims had in mind, it suits our family just fine.

Candied Sweet Potatoes

2 tablespoons butter or
  margarine
5 pounds sweet potatoes
½ teaspoon salt
Paprika
1½ cups dark brown sugar,
  firmly packed

Grated rind of 1 lemon
3 tablespoons lemon juice
⅓ cup orange juice
⅓ cup Grand Marnier
  (optional)
1 stick butter or margarine

Preheat the oven to 350 degrees with the rack in the center position. Butter an ovenproof baking dish large enough to hold the sweet potatoes. Peel the sweet potatoes and cut them into ½-inch slices and layer the slices in the prepared baking dish. Sprinkle with the salt and paprika. Combine the remaining ingredients in a saucepan and bring to a boil. Pour this mixture over the potatoes. Cover the dish with foil and bake for ½ hour. Uncover and bake for another ½ hour, basting frequently with the pan juices.

Serves 10–12

Deep-Dish Apple Pie

This recipe is easy to prepare and great for a crowd.

2 tablespoons butter or
  margarine
6–8 large-sized Cortland
  apples, peeled, cored, and
  thinly sliced
1 cup sugar

2 tablespoons flour
Pinch of salt
1 tablespoon cinnamon
4 tablespoons butter or
  margarine

Preheat the oven to 450 degrees with the rack in the center position. Use the 2 tablespoons of butter to grease a 9 × 13-inch ovenproof dish. Layer the apples in the dish. Combine the sugar, flour, salt, and cinnamon and sift this mixture over the apples. Let stand at room temperature while you prepare the crumb topping.

FOR THE CRUMB TOPPING

½ cup sugar
⅓ cup flour
¼ cup (four tablespoons)
  butter or margarine, softened

1 teaspoon cinnamon
¾ cup finely chopped walnuts

Combine all the above ingredients and sprinkle over the apples. Bake at 450 degrees for 15 minutes and then lower oven to 350. Bake an additional 45 minutes.

Serves 10

Reading at the Table

No matter how carefully a parent approaches the subject of food, the truth is that many children would rather do almost anything else than eat. This is why kids like to read at the table. If you don't have to give your full attention to pickled beets or broiled liver (that still looks and tastes exactly like broiled liver no matter how tiny you cut the pieces up and mush it together with your potatoes), then somehow the food goes down easier. Most adults (although many are loath to admit it) love to read at the table as well. What a supremely comforting feeling it is to select your own company and have them behave exactly the way you want. When you tire of the company simply change the book. No pressure to make trivial conversation, no awkward silences or looks of disapproval when you slurp your soup or drop a dressing-soaked glop of lettuce onto your lap.

How I treasure those lunches down at my local coffee shop when it's just me, the latest Dick Francis, and an overstuffed BLT (brisket, lettuce, and tomato) on toast washed down with a raspberry lime rickey. And I'll bet I'm not the only one who has heated up last night's macaroni and cheese and absentmindedly stained the centerfold of the latest *Gourmet* as I ogled the dinner of the month. How could a practice that gives so much pleasure be frowned upon so severely by those in the manners racket?

I was delighted some years ago to see that picture of young Amy Carter sitting at a fancy White House dinner, her elbow on the table, her chin resting in her hand, and her attention entirely absorbed by the book in front of her. There she was—the First Child—validating what I had always held dear and true—that it's OK to read at the table, even at state dinners. My parents, who saw this permissiveness as yet another opportunity to condemn the Carter administration, let me read at the table only when I was eating alone—and certainly never at state dinners. I'll bet if Eleanor Roosevelt had read at state dinners I could have too.

During my grammar school years I came home for lunch. I made it my business to stop at the school library in the free time before class so that I could pick up a book to take home at noon. Kindergarten and first grade saw a constant stream of *Curious George*, Dr. Seuss, and *The Five Chinese Brothers* ad nauseam. In third grade I devoured the entire set of *The Bobbsey Twins*. Every day from 12:15 to 12:45 I shared the sunny, untroubled lives of Freddy and Flossie and Burt and Nan. My mother would warn me that I was going to be late for school, but I would sit there in my Amy Carter pose, cream of tomato (Campbell's, made with half milk, half light cream) mustache on my upper lip, dreamily munching on Ritz crackers slathered with cream cheese, while I romped down the streets of fantasyville dodging that no-good Danny Ruggles.

In fourth grade, between bites of tuna fish sandwich (Bumblebee, if you please, with Hellmann's mayonnaise, finely chopped celery, Wonder Bread, crusts off, cut into four triangles) and milk (with a chocolate Flavor Straw), I spent my life with the Melendy family in Elizabeth Enright's wonderful series that included *The Saturdays*, *The Four Story Mistake*, and *Spider Web For Two*. My friends Mona, Rush, Randy, and Oliver took me far away from bitter winds that chapped the backs of my legs on the walk back to school. I wasn't cold. I was finding arrowheads in the summer fields and putting on plays in the parlor to make money to buy war bonds. I loved those books so much that I still keep them on the bookshelf near my bed and pick them up to read even now, both to my children and to myself. In between the Melendy stories I read and reread several hundred volumes of *Nancy Drew*. While my teacher turned up her nose at such lightweight fare and would not allow them as material for book reports, I spent countless bologna (Gulden's mustard, soft onion roll) sandwich lunches dreaming of the day when, like Nancy, I could wear a frock (whatever that was) and drive a coupe.

My fifth grade infatuation with the *Black Stallion* and his endless adventures didn't last terribly long. No, I gave up on horses early and got right into nurses. *Clara Barton, R.N.* kept me enthralled through endless grilled cheese sandwiches (white American, not yellow, and the sandwich had to be pressed down really hard in the pan so that the cheese melted and squished out and got brown and crunchy). Mom, who thought I needed fattening up, made me thick frappes with lots of Hershey's syrup and two scoops of coffee ice cream. The medical field held me for a while until I discovered *Junior Miss* by Sally Bensen. This book just tickled my fancy. I must have checked it out of the library at least once a week for most of my time in the fifth grade. I loved reading about this girl (sort of like me, I liked to imagine) who was coming of age in New York City. She and her snooty sister, Lois, had sophisticated adventures involving boys that made me decide that right after lunch, I was moving to New York.

In sixth grade I discovered romance and gothic novels. I also finally had permission to use the adult section of the public library. I lugged home hefty volumes like *Rebecca* and *Gone with the Wind*, and ate cream cheese and jelly sandwiches while I tossed my hair in the ocean breeze or danced with Rhett in a dress that showed off my ample bust and tiny waist. My mother said that like violinists who get permanent bruises on their necks from the constant rubbing of their instruments, I would have a lifelong callous on the side of my chin from resting my head in my hand while I read. That was fine with me. While other girls were hysterically pondering the terrors of life beyond the sixth grade, I found out from my books all there was to know about men and romance. [I picked up a copy of *Gone with the Wind* a while ago and was overwhelmed by the need to eat saltines with crunchy peanut butter while I read. Then I realized that was the very thing I ate while I read the book the first time.]

When I got to junior high school we didn't get to go home for lunch anymore. I had to confine my reading at the table to the evenings when my parents would go out. There was an added bonus to these evenings. Besides being able to choose my own company, my mother made me my favorite guilt meal—that's her guilt at leaving me all alone to eat dinner while they went out. This was the guilt meal menu: two extra thick rib lamb chops broiled black on the outside and still pink on the inside, mashed potatoes made with tons of heavy cream and butter, canned baby peas, and for dessert chocolate pudding with a thick layer of heavy cream on the top. Maybe my mother felt guilty, but I loved it when they went out. First of all I got this great food, and secondly I got to read all the dirty books they thought they had hidden so well. Yessiree. My dad thought I was gobbling up the entire set of Samuel Eliot Morison's *Admiral of the Ocean Sea*. Little did they suspect that as soon as they pulled out of the driveway I was on my hands and knees rummaging around on the floor of their closet, behind my father's shoes. I always hit pay dirt. I got to read *Peyton Place* in the hardcover edition while all my friends had to wait until it came out in paperback. I savored my lamb chops along with the seamy adventures of that horny Rodney Harrington and that goody two shoes, Allison MacKenzie. Remember *The Bramble Bush*? I read and reread that book over countless dishes of chocolate pudding. Hell, I even got to read *The Tropic of Cancer*, but I didn't get most of it. *A Stone For Danny Fisher* was more my speed.

In high school I discovered Philip Roth. I read *Goodbye, Columbus* over pizza, with meatball heroes, and hundreds, no thousands, of tuna melts. No longer did I want to be Nancy Drew and drive a coupe. I wanted to be Brenda Patimkin and belong to a country club, get a nose job, and go to Radcliffe. I didn't get too far; the only resemblance I had to Brenda was that we too had a refrigerator full of fruit in the basement. Then I went through a long Willa Cather and Ernest Hemingway phase when I don't remember at all what I ate, but I spoke in short, uncluttered sentences and had cluttered, confusing dreams about big game fishing in Nebraska.

I have a special bookshelf filled with volumes of my childhood favorites. Sometimes my children choose one of these to eat lunch with. More often they will find a book of their own, and more often than not, after they go back to school I find myself reading whatever they left behind on the table. Thus, I have enjoyed Beverly Cleary (with a Greek salad) and Judy Blume (with leftover pasta). The other day I found my little guy (only four years old) at the dining room table, sitting on his knees so he could comfortably assume that traditional posture of the chin in the hand, elbow on the table, eating the last bite of his peanut butter and jelly sandwich, totally engrossed in *Green Eggs and Ham*. That's my boy.

Homemade Cream of Tomato Soup

It's not quite as easy as opening a can, but the results are well worth it!

1 large Spanish onion, chopped
3 tablespoons vegetable oil
3 cloves garlic, minced
¼ cup fresh dill, chopped
1 28-ounce can peeled, whole tomatoes or canned pureed tomatoes or the same amount of fresh, very flavorful tomatoes in season, peeled, chopped, and seeded
2 tablespoons honey

5 cups chicken stock, either homemade or commercially prepared (such as College Inn), or vegetable soup base— see note below
1 tablespoon Worcestershire sauce
Salt, white pepper to taste
Few drops Tabasco sauce
1½ cups heavy cream (see note below on low-fat version)
Fresh, chopped scallions

In a heavy-bottomed 3-quart pot, sauté the onions in the oil until they are lightly browned and translucent. Add the garlic and cook over low heat for several minutes, taking care not to let the garlic brown. Stir in the dill, the tomatoes, and the honey. Mix well and cook over moderate heat for 5 minutes. Add the stock and bring to a low boil. Lower the heat, cover, and simmer for 1 hour.

Add the Worcestershire sauce and then the salt, pepper, and Tabasco to taste. Cool slightly and then puree in small batches in a food processor or blender. Return to the pot and add the heavy cream (or yogurt). Correct the seasoning and heat to serving temperature without boiling. Garnish with chopped scallions.

Serves 8–10

NOTE

You can substitute low-fat plain yogurt for the heavy cream. The taste will be tangier but still delicious. Take care not to boil the soup once the yogurt has been added.

Vegetable soup base can be made by mixing 1 cube Knorr's vegetable bouillon in 2 cups boiling water.

Grilled Cheese Sandwich

Yes, Virginia, there is an art to making the quintessential grilled cheese sandwich. Let's start with the bread; my favorite is Pepperidge Farm whole wheat. It has substance and flavor yet it obligingly flattens when it is supposed to without falling apart. OK, now the cheese; I like Land O Lakes American white, but my mother-in-law, Ida Brody of West Hartford, Connecticut, uses only yellow Velveeta and makes one hell of a great grilled cheese sandwich. You may want to add a slice of tomato or a slice of Bermuda onion. The only other ingredients you need are butter and bread and butter pickle slices and you're in business.

1 tablespoon butter	1 slice tomato or 1 slice
2 slices Pepperidge Farm	Bermuda onion
whole wheat bread	Bread and butter pickle slices
3 slices white American cheese	

Place the butter in a small saucepan and heat it until it is sizzling. Quickly place 1 slice of bread in the pan, just long enough to coat it with butter and then remove it. Add the other slice of bread, cover with the cheese and the optional tomato and/or onion, then top with the other slice of bread, butter side up. Use a flat pan cover or metal spatula to press down very hard on the sandwich (my mother-in-law puts the whole thing in an electric waffle iron with removable grids). When the bottom is browned, flip the sandwich over and repeat on the other side. The sandwich should be very flat, and some of the cheese may run out and get brown—this is good, it tastes delicious. Serve immediately with bread and butter pickle slices.

Makes 1 sandwich

Campbell's Cream of Tomato Soup
—and Then Some

If the Campbell's Soup Company had a contest for all the things one could do to what I think is already an almost perfect product, I would surely be given some sort of prize. Since this soup was one of the mainstays of my childhood diet, my mother cautiously used it to get me to branch out and try other kinds of foods. The following is a list of our family's variations on this canned classic; all the extras were added once the basic soup was made from one can of whole milk for every can of soup. If you want to use a meat garnish, use water instead of milk.

- Garnish with sour cream or plain yogurt and a sprinkling of paprika or cayenne.
- Place a generous tablespoon of grated sharp cheddar in the bottom of each individual bowl before adding the hot soup.
- Add dried oregano and sprinkle with grated Parmesan cheese.
- Add Monterey Jack or herbed jalapeno pepper cheese, chili powder to taste, and garnish with broken-up Doritos.
- Top with several crushed Ritz crackers.
- Top with grated Swiss cheese and run under the broiler before serving.
- Cook with several sprigs of fresh cilantro, dill, or thyme, or add a pinch of those herbs dried.
- Top with chopped hard-cooked egg.
- Add diced smoked turkey.
- Add a dash of Tabasco or A.1. Steak Sauce and sprinkle with fresh chopped parsley.
- Blend in 3 tablespoons of heavy cream, yogurt, or sour cream mixed with 2 tablespoons of Dijon mustard.
- Add chunks of fresh (in season) ripe tomatoes and crumbled dried basil.

- Toast rounds of French bread, spread with butter, sprinkle with grated cheese, and float on top of each cup of soup.

And finally, a rather strange-sounding but delicious-tasting combination:

- Top with crumbled blue cheese and herbed croutons.

Enough already!

The Perfect Jewish Bologna Sandwich

Everyone in the movie theater snickered with derision when Annie Hall asked for a pastrami sandwich on white bread with mayonnaise. Woody Allen knew that true mavens would see humor in dressing the ultimate Jewish meat in WASP clothing. One has to be just as careful when dealing with bologna; here's what to do: smear a bulky roll (onion or poppy seed is fine) with mustard. Now, I'm talking American mustard, the kind that you squirt on hot dogs at the ball game—save the fancy French stuff for your paté sandwiches. Next pile about 1½ inches of kosher bologna on the bottom half of the roll. A skinny sandwich has all the appeal of an anorexic in an oversized fur coat. On top of the bologna put a couple of leaves of iceberg lettuce—this gives some crunch to the bite—then top with the other half of the roll and enjoy. (I was so used to eating this sandwich out of a lunch bag that it just didn't taste right if it wasn't flattened by whatever else was in the bag too.)

A Premier Tuna Fish Sandwich

I know, I know—you're not supposed to call it tuna FISH because that's redundant. Well, to hell with redundancy, tuna FISH is what I called it then, and tuna FISH is what I call it now. As long as we understand one another . . .

1 7-ounce can Bumblebee (my favorite) solid white tuna packed in oil	1 small sweet onion, finely chopped (optional)
Several large tablespoons Hellmann's mayonnaise	4 slices lightly toasted light rye, sissle, corn rye, or pumpernickel bread
2 large celery stalks (preferably the light, tender, yellow green stalks from the inside of the bunch), finely minced	Additional mayonnaise
	Iceberg lettuce
	Dill pickle spears
	Wise potato chips

Place the tuna fish in a large wooden bowl and mash it with a fork or a metal chopper. Stir in the mayonnaise and then the celery and onion, if desired. Spread the toasted bread with some mayonnaise, mound a generous amount of tuna fish on 2 slices of bread, cover with lettuce, and top with the remaining bread. Serve with pickles and potato chips.

Makes 2 sandwiches

Tuna Melt

This variation is heaven, indeed. Turn the broiler on high or use a toaster oven set on top broil. After you place the tuna on the bread, cover it with several thin, overlapping slices of Swiss or cheddar (harder to get thinner slices) cheese. Broil until the cheese melts, add a slice of tomato, if you wish, some lettuce, and enjoy!

Chocolate Coffee Frappe

In Connecticut this was called a milk shake, in Rhode Island it's called (for some strange reason) a cabinet, here in Massachusetts it's known as a frappe. Under any name, it's delicious!

8 ounces whole milk
1 scoop coffee (or better yet,
   coffee fudge) ice cream
3 tablespoons chocolate syrup

Place all the ingredients in a blender and blend until frothy.

Makes 1 frappe

Down the Beach:
The Sand Castle Years

While the Connecticut shoreline is not the Costa del Sol, the warm and gentle waters of the Long Island Sound drew us like a sunny, sandy magnet each summer of my childhood. Small towns, each with their distinctive personality, lined the shore route offering a different sort of vacation within the greater experience of being away from the city; away to the beach—or down the beach, as we used to say.

When I was very young my Aunt Sarah would take me for a week in July to a three-decker, wooden beachfront hotel in Niantic. We would travel there with her friend Anna Smith (Tante Anna to me) and Anna's niece Janie, who was around my age. The beauty of this hotel was that it was ideally located, for my aunt and her friend didn't drive and cabs were scarce as crab's teeth.

My memories of the beach itself are dim; bottle green murky water, sandbars giving up secrets of shells and tiny dried-out crabs that I would put in my pail to take home to the city, but what I do recollect with crystal clarity is the adventure of the diner where we took all our meals. The idea of eating three meals a day in a restaurant was heaven to a six-year-old who felt she had no control over what her mother laid down on the table. My Aunt Sarah could have cared less that I wanted to eat the same thing day after day, or that I never ate a vegetable all week, or that Janie and I used the paper straws to blow bubbles in our chocolate milk. She and tante sat, smoking Lucky Strikes and gossiping, only stopping to reprimand us if we interrupted the other patrons' peace and quiet.

The walk to the diner took us out the door of our hotel, across the main street down two short blocks, across some railroad tracks, and through the minute village (post office, gas station, and hardware store). The diner, deep blue with silver trim on the outside, sat at an oblique angle to the railroad tracks. Inside, the lower half of the walls was paneled with dark wood with windows above. The benches below the wooden tables were covered with red vinyl that, in the very hot weather, made it hard to slide over when you were wearing shorts or a damp bathing suit. We always sat at the same table at the very back of the diner under a large window that afforded an exceedingly close-up view of the railroad tracks. We always had the same waitress. Keeping with this theme, I usually ordered the same thing: breakfast— orange juice, soft scrambled eggs, white toast dripping with butter; lunch—tuna sandwich on white bread, extra pickles, and chocolate milk; dinner—grilled cheese sandwich on white bread (I loved that white bread), extra pickles, chips, chocolate milk, and chocolate ice cream for dessert. While the food was at best unthreatening and the price was right, the thing Janie and I really loved about the diner was that at least once during every meal the train between Boston and New York City would pass with an earsplitting roar within several feet of our window. No matter how many times we saw that train, no matter how accustomed we were to its monumental racket, we still felt its reverberating presence in the pit of our stomachs; something to be feared and loved all at once. Its nearness was simply terrifying.

The summer I was nine my mother, brother, and I were invited to spend a week at a beach house owned by one of my father's cousins. My memories of that week are of women— mothers, aunts, older cousins—wearing aprons (to keep their housedresses clean), doing chores, and complaining, "This is not a vacation for me!" Between shopping and cooking and laundry and sweeping the ever-present sand out of the house and minding the kids who, their mothers were sure, were intent on drowning themselves in the Long Island Sound, the women wore themselves to a frazzle. No wonder my father (and all the other men) came only on weekends and then immediately retreated (with collapsible beach chair and a fat novel) to the far reaches of the beach completely out of earshot of the overworked women. My mother was martyred that week; while she was doing the hundredth load of wash she got her hand caught in the manual ringer of the tub washer. She panicked and instead of reversing the rollers, managed to roll her fingers through to the knuckle. Her fingers swelled up like fat sausages and she was absolved from further household jobs. She spent the rest of the week resting her Mercurochrome-painted fingers on the edge of a beach chair in the backyard.

The kids hit the beach practically at sunrise and had to be dragged home kicking and screaming at the end of the day. We built elaborate sand structures with moats and fortifications. We buried each other up to our chins in great handfuls of heavy, wet sand that got into our eyes and underneath our bathing suits, making us squirm with the itchies. We had mud fights with the boy cousins, and we spent endless hours pickling ourselves in the briny water until the female person in charge would look up from her knitting or gin rummy hand and yell, "Come out right now, your lips are purple." We would hop up and down, shivering with cold, clutching our thin arms around our waterlogged bodies while the mother (aunt, grandmother, or elder cousin) wrapped us in faded beach towels.

I cannot remember any hunger quite as acute and demanding as the one that overcame me after several hours hard at play on the beach. From the depths of the cooler would come three-decker peanut butter and banana sandwiches, juicy plums bursting with summer's sweetness, and lemon/limeaid made my mother's very special way. We passed around a big bag of Wise potato chips and licked the greasy, salty crumbs off our already salted and sanded fingers. There was usually a foil-covered paper plate loaded with crumbly brownies or oatmeal-raisin cookies that disappeared instantly. After lunch we lounged around on our towels until the heat of the sun either put us to sleep or drove us back into the waves.

Back at the house at the end of the afternoon we sat on the picnic table in the backyard waiting our turn for the outdoor shower. One at a time we entered the shack attached to the end of the porch, carefully latching the door and covering up the peephole the boys had strategically gouged in the wall. Stepping carefully to avoid the soggy grass between the floorboards I would then strip off my bathing suit and check out how brown I had become that day. The first few days at the beach I had become so red and stiff that I had shivered all night long from the touch of the sheets on my skin. By now, though, I was "looking like an Indian," as my aunt would say. It gave me a creepy feeling to be showering, naked, so close to the boys sitting on the bench right outside the door. They always teased that they were coming in if I took too long, so for that reason there was always a residue of sand in my hair until we returned home and my mother gave me a proper shampoo.

After supper, in clean shorts and shirts, we were allowed to return to the beach on the condition that we didn't go near the water. We would sit on the stone jetty, our toes in the tide pools ducking the advances of curious sand crabs, watching the enormous orange red sun sink lower and lower into the sound and wait for the first fireflies to appear. Later, entombed in their glass peanut butter jar prisons placed on the dresser near my bed the fireflies, winking their faint golden lights, danced their last dance just for me. The gentle lapping of the waves, punctuated by an occasional distant foghorn, lulled me to sleep.

Lemon Limeade

We like this really sweet, but you can cut back the sugar if you prefer the pucker of citrus.

1 cup granulated sugar	Juice and pulp of 2 limes
4 cups water	1 lemon, sliced and seeded
Juice and pulp (but not seeds) of 4 lemons	1 lime, sliced

Place the sugar and 1 cup of the water in a small saucepan and bring the mixture to a boil, stirring just until the sugar dissolves completely. Cool slightly and then pour into a pitcher. Stir in the lemon and lime juices and the pulp. Add the remaining water (it should be very cold). Another version of this can be made by adding 3 cups of sparkling water instead of still water. Add the lemon and lime slices to the pitcher and serve over ice.

Makes 1½ quarts, approximately

Peanut Butter and Banana Sandwiches

My cousins David and Mark Apter from Washington, D.C., introduced these to me when we were kids at the beach. Over the years I forgot about them and was reintroduced at, of all places, Canyon Ranch, the luxury health and fitness spa in Tucson, Arizona. A group of us had just finished a strenuous sunrise trail bike ride through Sabino Canyon and we were ravenous. From out of his pack our leader pulled a stack of peanut butter and banana sandwiches. The uninitiated among us started to turn up their noses at such pedestrian fair. I, on the other hand, knowing full well the delicious treat in store made a lusty grab for mine and chowed down. The others quickly followed suit.

4 tablespoons crunchy peanut butter (the natural style or freshly ground kind is preferable)

4 thick slices of whole grain bread
1 ripe banana

Spread 1 tablespoon of peanut butter on each slice of bread. Slice the banana and divide the slices on top of 2 pieces of bread. Top with the other slice of bread. If you are going to eat the sandwich right away, toasting the bread makes it even more delicious.

Oatmeal-Raisin Cookies

1½ sticks (6 ounces) butter
1 cup dark brown sugar,
  firmly packed
½ cup granulated sugar
1 extra large egg
¼ cup water
2 teaspoons vanilla extract
1 cup all-purpose flour,
  measured after sifting
1 teaspoon cinnamon
½ teaspoon nutmeg
½ teaspoon ginger
½ teaspoon cloves
½ teaspoon baking soda
1½ cups golden raisins
1 cup (5–6 ounces) walnuts or
  pecans broken into large
  pieces
3 cups *quick cooking* oats

Preheat the oven to 350 degrees with the rack in the center position. Line 3 heavy-duty cookie sheets with foil, or grease and dust them with flour. Either by hand or with an electric mixer set on slow speed, cream the butter, sugars, egg, water, and vanilla. Resift the flour together with the spices and baking soda and add to the mixture. Mix in the raisins, nuts, and oats. Use a soupspoon to form mounds and set them 1½ inches apart on the cookie sheets. Bake for 12–14 minutes, reversing the rack back to front once during baking. Cool the cookies on a wire rack and repeat with the remaining cookie sheets.

If you find the bottoms are burning before the tops are done, slip another cookie sheet underneath the first.

These cookies freeze beautifully. I store them in heavy-duty zip-lock plastic bags in the freezer.

Makes about 4 dozen

Doughnuts and Coppertone

Toward the end of junior high I was old enough to go on my own to visit my friends whose parents rented places down the beach. The beach of choice for me was Sound View. It was the personification of honky-tonk, but it had boys, an arcade, and the best doughnuts this side of heaven.

Cheaply constructed, ancient, ramshackle cottages (built where no architect had gone before) were jammed together, with after-thought additions clinging to dubious second floors. Precariously perched cantilevered gables were flung helter-skelter on already crowded rooflines, and around the back tiny shacks (for the bubbe to stay in) sprang up like mushrooms in postage-stamp yards. Most of the cottages had porches from which the street traffic could be readily observed and where the refrigerator was usually kept—since there was never enough room in the kitchen itself.

Extended matriarchal families comprised of *the* mother, her children, her mother (the bubbe), several aunts and their children (the cousins) shared dark narrow rooms crowded with lumpy beds (with white painted brass headboards) covered with thin stain-ed mattresses that always smelled of mildew. The shrill sounds of women screaming at children to eat, clean up, get out from underfoot, drove *the* father to commute on weekends (from Hart-ford or New Haven) and *the* grandfather (zayde) to spend every waking hour out of the house playing pinochle with the other zaydes.

The beach itself was wall-to-wall people: fat bubbes with sun-leathered skin and thighs as big around as their waists standing hip deep in the water splashing water on their bosoms so the shock of the cold wouldn't stop their hearts; skinny brown boys, all legs and arms like smooth spiders, in flapping wet trunks, throwing balls to each other across families gathered around beach blankets rigged with towel tents protecting young babies' tender skin; groups of mothers, watching with one eye while their children swam ("Hey Mom! Watch me float!") and the other on a bridge hand or the latest issue of *McCall's*. The beach was permeated with the smell of cocoa butter, which everyone applied in liberal amounts hoping to achieve a tan that would last them until next summer. My friends and I either greased up with Coppertone or we smeared ourselves with a mixture of Johnson's baby oil and Mercurochrome. (Plastic surgeons and oncologists are now, undoubtedly, trying to undo the ravages of that bit of insanity.)

I have a snapshot of our gang from that summer. I flinch when I see myself in a bubble hairdo (hours of sleepless nights on the metal rollers, my hair slicked down with Jokur), decked out in a bathing suit that came equipped with an instant bust; those hollow foam cups that jutted out from my bony chest giving me the profile of Olive Oyl. God forbid that you forgot for one moment and lay down on your stomach on your beach towel—when you sat up your breasts would have dents in them, which caused all the boys to poke each other and scream with laughter. You couldn't put Kleenex in there in case one of the boys threw you in the water, and you were constantly giving sly looks downward to make sure that your bust hadn't migrated to one side or another and was still lined up the way it should be.

After we girls staked out our territory with our beach towels, we would oil ourselves and then walk up and down the length of the beach at water level waiting to see who would notice us. You could tell when a boy noticed you because he splashed you with water. You screamed and got angry in response. You then stormed back to your towel. If he was really serious he would come over and sit on your towel too (his soggy bathing suit making a damp, sandy spot). To be more accurate, he didn't just come right over and plop himself down. What would happen is first he and his buddies would throw their ball over in the direction of your towel. Then they would run over, pick it up, and manage to spray you and everyone else in the area with sand. This would happen three or four times, each time the ball got closer to the towel, each time the sand shower got worse, and each time the people who were getting sprayed yelled louder until someone yelled, "Sit down or get out of here, for Christ sake!" Then and only then would he sit on the blanket. So, there the two of you were (well, actually the two of you and your six girlfriends), sitting on your blanket watching the water drip down his skinny legs, him trying to guess if you were really as stacked as you looked, you trying not to notice that you could see his jockstrap peeping out from under the top of his bathing suit. For a while we would listen to Brenda Lee wailing about being sorry on someone's transistor radio interspersed with the eight-year-old Stein twins whining on the next blanket. Then he might offer to rub some suntan glop on your back or suggest going to get a Coke at the arcade. If your girlfriends were real friends they would not get up and walk with the two of you toward the arcade. If they turned out to be self-serving bitches, then you would find yourself going out on a date with six chaperones.

The arcade, housed in a long wooden firetrap in the center of town, was filled with pinball machines and other games of chance that took your money and gave you a two-minute rush of adrenalin in return. It smelled and sounded just like every other arcade in the world—bells, beeps, dingers and gongs, pool balls clucking, the rolling swoosh of bowling balls. The ground was sticky with spilled soda, carelessly discarded gum, and cigarette butts. Since the arcade had no ventilation except the open door to the street, there was the usual kaleidoscope of smells: the buttery smell of fresh popcorn mingling with cotton candy, the thick and heavy addition of unfiltered cigarette smoke, as well as the sweet and unexpected undercurrent of Canoe cologne and Old Spice after-shave.

Aside from the neon glow of the pinball machines there was little other illumination, and all the corners of the room receded into pockets of mysterious blackness. The young pool sharks in the back had to squint mightily to spot their next moves. It was strange to make the sudden transition from brilliant summer beach daylight to the murky netherworld of the arcade. My mother and aunts had warned me that there were sailors there and I should look out for them. I suddenly would feel very nervous about my counterfeit chest and tell the boy that I would rather have a doughnut instead. If he had any sense at all he would agree because the handmade doughnuts from the open-air shop next to the arcade set the standard for any other doughnut to be found anywhere in the world.

The doughnut shop was open only as long as there were doughnuts to be sold. There were never any left over either in the shop after the first rush or in the bags brought home. The shelf life of these ethereal morsels was about half an hour. Early in the morning (especially on weekends when they had been looking for an excuse to get out of the house since dawn and the first baby's cry) the fathers and grandfathers and uncles would line up to buy dozens of jelly doughnuts so exquisitely light and tender that they barely held the fillings in: lemon, tart and sweet; raspberry that made your mouth pucker; and (my favorite) blueberry, with its thick, warm, lumpy blue-purple filling. They were dusted with powdered sugar that left even the most fastidious eater with a fine white mustache. The raised (honey dipped) doughnuts were legendary—their sweet white glaze still soft and warm from the kitchen. I also had a special affinity for the French crullers. Firstly, I liked the name—it sounded pretty cosmopolitan—and then I loved the gummy insides full of air holes, the sort of rubbery texture, and the white, sugary icing. The doughnut shop closed after the initial morning rush and then reopened around lunchtime and then again after supper. I could have happily lived on nothing but doughnuts my week down the beach. I never did stop to think how the bubbes grew their thighs so thick.

If the romance were meant to go somewhere after the doughnut (or Coke), the boy might ask if I were going to be hanging out that night. That meant would I be cruising the arcade or main street. Since I was only allowed to visit nice girls (approved of by my parents) I was never allowed to cruise anywhere but the cottage at night. The trick was, at that point, to get him to agree to drop by your friend's house. He would be noncommittal, of course, since he had to see if his buddies had anything better planned. If he showed he showed.

That evening, after agonizing for hours about what to wear to conceal the fact that my bathing suit had a figure of its own, I might settle down with the girls on the front porch of the cottage for a game of canasta (punctuated by fits of high, squeaky, nervous giggles), ever vigilant to the footsteps of passersby. Amidst the sharp clop, clop of Cuban heels, the flop of leather sandals, and the click of loafers with taps on the toes, I was listening for the quiet pad of high-top basketball sneakers. More often than not my Sound View Romeo would show up around ten, around the time my host's mother would be yelling down for us to get ready for bed. A few shy words would be exchanged over the porch railing, and then I would have to say good night and maybe we would meet on the beach tomorrow.

Up in my room in the lumpy bed, Noxzema smeared all over my face and the pink plastic rollers lacerating my scalp, I could hear the distant hurdy-gurdy noise of the arcade mixed with the slaps of the cards and grunts of the losers of the card game on the next porch. The zayde's cigars drew arcs of burning red as they gestured to their cronies with quick, sweeping movements. A cranky baby complained, and the exhausted pad of slippered feet climbed the stairs one more time (the mother muttering, ''This is no vacation for me. . .'') and cigar smoke carried by the ocean breeze drifted through the window, the shade flapping with each soft breath. As I shifted and squirmed to get comfortable, trying to ignore the sand in my bed, the sunburn on my back, and the pricks of pain in my scalp, I reflected on this perfect summer day down the beach, tomorrow morning's doughnuts, the possibility of a new boyfriend. Oh, if only it could be summer every day.

Raised Doughnuts

I am convinced that it is impossible to replicate exactly the doughnuts that are made in bakeries and doughnut shops where commercial equipment is used. Since consistency of the dough and the temperature of the fat are such key elements in the success of doughnuts, and since these elements are so difficult to control at home, the results are never consistently up to the standards of my memory. However, this recipe (one my mother has used for years) comes pretty close. The important thing is to pay attention to the temperature of the fat (a fat thermometer—also called a frying thermometer—is necessary).

1 cup milk, scalded and then cooled to lukewarm
3 tablespoons granulated sugar
¼ ounce (one package) dry yeast
3½ cups flour, sifted before measuring, plus additional flour for rolling
½ teaspoon salt
¼ teaspoon allspice
¼ teaspoon nutmeg
2 extra large eggs
4 tablespoons butter, melted and slightly cooled
¾ cup granulated sugar
Vegetable oil for frying
Confectioners sugar

Place the milk and sugar in a small bowl and sprinkle the yeast over it. Stir to dissolve the yeast and set aside. Resift the flour together with the salt and spices. Combine the yeast mixture with 2 cups of the flour, mix very well, cover the bowl, and let rise in a warm place until doubled in volume. Beat the eggs and add them, the melted butter, and the sugar to the batter and mix very well. Recover the bowl and let the dough rise again until doubled in volume. Punch down and place on a well-floured board and knead in a bit more flour until the dough can be rolled without sticking. Roll the dough out to a thickness of ½ inch and use a floured doughnut cutter to cut out about 2 dozen doughnuts. Carefully transfer the doughnuts to a lightly floured baking sheet and let them rise, uncovered, for 45 minutes to one hour. Heat the oil in a deep skillet or heavy kettle to a depth of 4 inches. Insert a fat thermometer and heat the oil to between 365–375 degrees. Cooking only 3 at a time, place the doughnuts in the hot oil with a metal slotted spoon. Cook for about 3 minutes on each side or until they are golden brown on both sides, adding more oil if necessary. Drain well on several thicknesses of paper towels, then dust generously with confectioners sugar.

Makes about 2 dozen doughnuts

Buttermilk Cake Doughnuts

When making any fried pastry it is essential to use a fat thermometer.

4½ cups flour, sifted before measuring, plus additional flour for rolling the doughnuts
¼ teaspoon cinnamon
¼ teaspoon ginger
¼ teaspoon nutmeg
1½ teaspoons baking soda
1½ teaspoons cream of tartar
½ teaspoon salt
3 extra large eggs
½ cup light brown sugar
½ cup granulated sugar
3 tablespoons butter, melted
1 cup buttermilk
Vegetable oil for frying

Resift the flour together with the spices, baking soda, cream of tartar, and salt. Place the eggs and brown and granulated sugars in the work bowl of an electric mixer and beat at high speed until the mixture is thick and light yellow in color. On low speed mix in the butter and buttermilk and then the flour. Continue mixing until the ingredients are well incorporated. Divide the dough in half, cover with plastic wrap, and chill for several hours.

Place enough vegetable oil in a deep skillet to make 4 inches of melted fat. Use a pastry thermometer to heat it to exactly 375 degrees. While the oil is heating roll out the dough on a very well-floured board to a thickness of ⅓ inch. Use a floured doughnut cutter to cut circles with holes in the center, or a 2-inch cookie cutter to cut just the "holes."

Fry the doughnuts 3 at a time for 2½ to 3 minutes on each side (until they are golden brown) then turn them with a metal slotted spoon to fry on the other side. Drain on several thicknesses of paper towels, then dust liberally with powdered sugar.

Makes about 3 dozen doughnuts

Canning Wars

The "other women" in my father's life were the Apple Lady, the Raspberry Lady, and the Peach Lady. These were our names for the owners of nearby tiny truck farms growing native produce who set aside the lion's share of their crops for my father, who was big into canning and freezing. My father would, sometime in the off-season, negotiate with the ladies for so many bushels of apples and peaches and so many pints of raspberries. When the crops were in the Peach Lady or the Apple Lady or the Raspberry Lady would phone, and the very next Saturday, right after breakfast, Mom and Dad would head over to the farm in the station wagon and return with a supermarket-sized load of fruit that we (the kids) would haul, basket after basket, into the kitchen where the canning (or freezing) wars would commence.

My father, the major general of the operation, would station himself midkitchen and shout directions to my mother and me (my brother would wisely vacate himself after he hauled in the last bushel basket), and we would at first frantically try to keep up with him and then gradually reduce the pace to one we could handle with a modicum of sanity. If we reduced it too much the general would bark an order to go faster. If we were making applesauce or canning peaches, then great blue enameled stockpots full of water were set to boil on the stove and glass canning jars were lined up on the counters.

The heavy golden- and rose-colored peaches were blanched and the fuzzy skins slipped off. Then they were sliced, cooked briefly in heavy sugar syrup, and then the slices were layered in the jars. Just before sealing Mom would stick in a peach pit— for flavor. The apples were halved and then cooked (skins and all to make the applesauce sweet and pink) slowly with very little liquid and some sugar and cinnamon, until they turned to mush. Mom would then run them through a Foley food mill, which dispensed of the skins and seeds, leaving a velvety smooth light-salmon-colored puree. This was spooned into canning jars. The jars were placed in metal racks and lowered into the sterilizer and boiled for the requisite number of minutes so that no one would get botulism. Then they were cooled and set to rest on the table, where they sat gleaming like the crown jewels. As they cooled, the metal caps would emit a gentle, random pop indicating that the suction created by the boiling had sealed the bottles. The steaming kettles spewed a warm, wet cinnamon-flavored mist into the air that steamed around the ceiling and onto our eyeglasses making it hard to see.

This operation was religiously accompanied at full blast by that Saturday afternoon's radio broadcast of the Metropolitan Opera's live matinee (brought to you by Texaco). Mom and I always performed with great efficiency to the energetic strains of Verdi and Puccini and less so to one of the more lugubrious, slow-paced composers like Wagner or someone obscure and hard to sing along to. Dad would get furious when we would want to sit down and take a break to listen to Texaco's opera quiz, which he considered a waste of effort since we rarely knew the answers to the obscure questions. At the end of the day, when Mom and I finally got to sit down, our feet no longer had any feeling and our backs were aching.

The raspberry harvest was treated in an altogether different manner since raspberries needed little processing and the longer they sat around the kitchen, the more they disappeared into the enemy's (those family members other than my father, the unabashed raspberry hoarder) mouths, leaving the bounty to be put up diminished by a few handfuls—an unforgivable thing in Dad's book.

Before he even went to pick up the berries, he would set out pint-sized plastic containers on the table. Once the flats of ruby redness were brought in he immediately got to work; this was no job for the lowly troops, only Dad could handle the processing of the berries. The peasants looked on with lust, trying to grab a few when the master's back was turned. Each container was filled almost to the top with berries. The fruit was never washed since this would make them mushy when they were defrosted, and how much harm can one or two small bugs do to you, anyway? The berries were topped off with a tablespoon of extra fine sugar, the lid snapped on, and then the container gently shaken to distribute the sugar. My father carefully labeled each container by year and then brought them down to the freezer, which in turn was locked with a small key that he kept in his pocket.

While my father was generous with the peaches, and the apple-sauce could be served anytime, it was the raspberries that one had to beg for. And they were worth it since there is nothing that gives you the courage to carry on through yet another icy February day like a dish of raspberries and heavy cream or a slice of my mom's raspberry streusel coffee cake. Not to discount the wonderful taste of those peaches topped with a scoop of vanilla ice cream or the heavenly velvetiness of the pink applesauce sitting beside some hot potato latkes at Chanukah.

I am happy to report that even though my brother and I are not there to be foot soldiers, the canning wars still go on. My father, the general, is a little slower carrying the mason jars and plastic containers up and down the basement steps and my mother sits while she peels the peaches, but the fruits and berries—the cream of the season's crops—get put up every summer, and every winter our whole family gets to enjoy them.

To Freeze Raspberries

Do not wash the raspberries! Immediately after they are picked (or bought), either spread them out on a tray and freeze, then gather them into zip-lock freezer bags for storage, or pile them into 1-pint plastic containers, leaving about 1 inch of headroom, and then sprinkle 1 tablespoon of extra fine sugar on top. Cover and shake gently, then freeze. The berries will hold their shape surprisingly well. Let them defrost in the bags or boxes. It is best to use them as soon as they defrost.

Raspberries and Cream

1 pint fresh or defrosted
   raspberries

1 cup (approximately)
   heavy cream
Fresh mint leaves

Divide the berries among 4 glasses—large red wine goblets are nice for this—and pour some heavy cream on top. Garnish with a fresh mint leaf.

Serves 4

Raspberry Streusel Coffee Cake

FOR THE STREUSEL

¼ cup dark brown sugar,
  firmly packed
¼ cup granulated sugar
1 teaspoon cinnamon

½ cup flour
½ cup chopped walnuts
4 tablespoons sweet (unsalted)
  butter

Combine the sugars and cinnamon in a small bowl. Mix in the flour and walnuts. Cut in the butter with a fork, or use your fingers to make the mixture into coarse crumbs.

FOR THE CAKE

2 sticks (8 ounces) sweet
  (unsalted) butter, at room
  temperature
1½ cups granulated sugar
2 extra large eggs
1½ cups sour cream
1 teaspoon vanilla

2½ cups flour, measured after
  sifting
1½ teaspoons baking powder
½ teaspoon salt
2 cups fresh or defrosted
  frozen raspberries strained
  of their juice

Preheat the oven to 350 degrees with the rack in the center position. Generously butter a 10-inch bundt pan or tube pan and dust it with flour, knocking out the excess flour.

In the bowl of an electric mixer cream together the butter and sugar until light and fluffy. Beat in the eggs, one at a time. Add the sour cream and vanilla and beat at medium speed for several minutes until the batter is light and well blended. Sift together the flour, the baking powder, and the salt. On slow speed add the dry ingredients mixing only until completely blended. Spread ½ of the cake batter in the bottom of the prepared pan. Sprinkle ½ the streusel over the batter. Evenly distribute half the raspberries over the streusel. Gently spread the remaining batter over the raspberries. Sprinkle the remaining raspberries and streusel on top and gently press down with a rubber scraper to make the top even.

Bake for 50–60 minutes or until the cake has started pulling away from the sides of the pan and a cake tester comes out dry. Make sure the top of the cake is firm to the touch. If it feels wet let it bake another few minutes.

When the cake is done, let it cool in the pan on a rack for 1 hour. Then invert and top with the following glaze.

FOR THE GLAZE

1 cup confectioners sugar	⅓ cup water
1 tablespoon lemon juice	⅓ cup finely chopped walnuts

Sift the sugar into a bowl. Mix in the lemon juice and then slowly dribble in the water, mixing until you have a thin paste. This glaze should be pourable but thick enough to coat the cake without being completely absorbed. Drizzle the glaze over the cake and then top with the walnuts.

Makes 1 10-inch cake

To Freeze Peaches

After years of slaving away over steaming kettles and wrestling with canning jars, my mother has discovered a much easier and equally flavorful way of preserving this delicate fruit. She maintains that this freezing method is superior to canning—and half the work! Since defrosted peaches tend to discolor faster than canned, it is important to use them immediately after defrosting.

TO MAKE 1 QUART

6–8 medium-sized ripe, flavorful, unblemished peaches
⅔ cup sugar

¼ teaspoon ascorbic acid or fresh fruit preserver (a commercially prepared product available in supermarkets), mixed in with the sugar
Juice of half a lemon

Bring a large pot of water to a boil. Turn off the heat and place the peaches in the water for about 3 minutes or just until the skin slips off. If the peaches are really ripe this will happen easily; if not peel the remaining skin off with a knife. Cut the peaches in half (or in quarters if you prefer) and place in a glass bowl. Sprinkle on the sugar/ascorbic acid mixture and shake the bowl to distribute. Let stand for about 10 minutes. Pack the peaches and any juice into a quart-sized plastic container or 2 pint-sized containers. Sprinkle the lemon juice on top. Seal. Shake the container once more and then freeze. Use immediately after defrosting.

Makes 1 quart

Applesauce

8–10 Cortland or McIntosh   ¾–1 cup sugar
    apples   ½ teaspoon cinnamon
1½ cups water or apple cider   Lemon juice to taste

Quarter the apples and remove the core and seeds (leave the skin on). Place the apples and water or cider in a deep, heavy-bottomed pot. Cook over low heat until the apples are very tender. Strain and reserve cooking liquid. Process the apples in a Foley food mill and add the remaining ingredients, including about ½–⅔ cup of the cooking liquid to taste.

Serves 8–10

Raspberry Applesauce

While it is slightly more delicious to make this simple recipe with homemade applesauce (see recipe on the preceding page) store-bought is perfectly acceptable. This makes a wonderful condiment to meat and poultry dishes.

1 10-ounce package frozen raspberries
1 quart applesauce

3 tablespoons framboise or other raspberry liqueur (optional)

Place the frozen berries in a coarse mesh sieve or strainer set over a bowl so that the juice runs off as the berries defrost. Discard the juice, replace the bowl under the sieve, and use a wooden spoon or stiff rubber spatula to push the berries through the sieve. Discard the seeds left in the sieve. Combine the pureed raspberries with the applesauce. Add the optional framboise, if desired.

Makes 8–10 servings

Broiled Peaches with Ginger and Brown Sugar

This is a particularly wonderful accompaniment to meat or game dishes such as rib roast or roast duck. It can also be served as dessert with a scoop of vanilla ice cream (see instructions below). Naturally it's best to use peaches that you have canned yourself (see recipe on page 89), failing that use the premium canned version.

8 skinless peach halves
1 tablespoon butter (for greasing the baking dish)
⅓ cup candied ginger
⅔ cup dark brown sugar, firmly packed

3 tablespoons butter or margarine
½ cup rum
½ cup orange juice

Preheat the oven to 350 degrees. Place the peaches, cavity or flat side up in one layer, in a buttered ovenproof baking dish. Use a chef's knife to chop the ginger by hand (a food processor won't work) until you have very fine pieces. Place the ginger and all the remaining ingredients in a small saucepan and cook over moderate heat, stirring occasionally until the sugar has melted and the mixture comes to a simmer. Mix well and pour over the peaches. Bake for 20 minutes or just until the peaches are hot.

To serve with a main course, place one peach half upside down on each plate and spoon some of the sauce into the pit cavity; or for dessert, place the peaches, cavity side up, in the bottom of individual serving bowls, place a scoop of vanilla ice cream on top, and then top with some of the sauce.

Serves 8

Peach Parfait with Raspberry Sauce

---

4 peach halves (home-canned or store bought)

1 pint best quality vanilla ice cream
Quick raspberry sauce (recipe follows)

Cut the peaches into spoon-sized chunks and place a few pieces at the bottom of each of 4 parfait glasses or wine goblets. Add a generous scoop of ice cream and top with the remaining peaches. Top with raspberry sauce.

Serves 4

Quick Raspberry Sauce

2½ cups fresh or previously frozen raspberries
½ cup extra fine sugar

¼ cup framboise or other raspberry liqueur (optional)

Place all the above ingredients in the work bowl of a blender or food processor and puree until smooth. If you want a slightly stronger flavor, add a couple of spoonfuls of raspberry preserve or a few drops of lemon juice.

Serves 4

Force-Feeding

Last week when I went to the butcher to buy pullets for my chicken soup, I waited in line to pay behind a lady who had a shopping basket filled with flat Styrofoam trays of steer liver. Another lady, behind me, looked around at the liver-loaded basket and winced. "My mother used to force that down my throat. Looking at it even now makes my stomach queasy." When I asked her what was that strange-looking meat in her basket, she replied, "Tongue." My stomach shuddered. This woman wouldn't eat liver, but she would eat tongue? Myself, I would die before I ate either one. You can include tripe in that category as well. Food is food and parts is parts, but organs are a part apart and that's where I draw the line. I am philosophically and gustatorially opposed to any food that has the consistency of rubber bands and has to be chewed and chewed and chewed some more and thus its origin continuously reflected upon by the chewer while the chewing is going on.

All my life I have happily gobbled up my mother's chopped liver (full of sautéed onions and hard-cooked egg, sprinkled with cracked pepper and kosher salt, moistened with rendered chicken fat, and slathered on fat slices of her freshly made challa). My thick head conveniently never made the connection between those repulsive dull maroon slabs of liver—liver steak my mother called it—and the delicious delicacy that graced our Friday night and holiday table. Even though they were both called "liver," I rationalized that the one I liked wasn't really liver at all but some other food that was called liver by accident. Sort of like eggplant (another food I wouldn't eat).

To say I was a picky eater is a gross understatement. My mother's war cry, echoed in millions of homes across the country where stubborn children sat facing down lima beans, stewed tomatoes, and little Pyrex dishes full of baked custard, was, "Some day you'll have a child as impossible as you and then you'll be sorry!" She was wrong. I had three children much worse than I was. I spent about five minutes being sorry and then just simply gave up. Since my mother with all her cajoling (One more spoonful for Grandma), guilt (I made this just for you), beseeching (Don't you want to grow up and be big and healthy?), threats (If you don't finish your carrots your brother will eat his tapioca pudding and yours too!), I never turned into a good eater during my childhood. So, if my kids wouldn't let a green vegetable pass between their lips; ate only predigested meat; wouldn't consider anything that came out of water a food source; demanded that I cut the crusts off their sandwiches, make toast without *any* brown spots, and brownies without nuts, I just sighed and did it. I knew some day they would learn how to eat delicious food—I knew from experience that it's not something someone can teach you or force on you.

So, I had my oatmeal (Irish, stone-ground, and made from scratch) with raisins, brown sugar, and a pat of sweet butter melting on top, and they ate instant glop that was made by pouring hot water over the contents of a package dumped into the bowl. I ate spinach fettuccine (cooked al dente) with herbs and garlic, and they ate shell noodles (mushy) with butter. They ate hamburgers and catsup and I ate steak tartar. Yes, I did a lot of extra cooking, but on the other hand, I never had to listen to the obnoxious dinnertime war cry of an unhappy child: "What is this junk?" and I rarely fed the disposal the contents of an untouched plate. Then one day, all on their own, one of their noses twitched at the irresistible fragrance of a duck breast sizzling on the grill. One pair of eyes watched hungrily while the butter melted into the plump golden raisins in my oatmeal, and one brave hand reached over and took a strand of pasta from my plate. Slowly but surely they came around. Now one loves sushi and another is devoted to hot and spicy Tex-Mex. The king of mashed potatoes and white bread developed a fondness for artichokes, asparagus, and sprouts.

So the kids became eaters, but in the tradition set by their mother, they have studiously avoided those "organic" chewy foods noted above. I often wonder, is it environment or genetics that has led them to love chopped liver (my mother's famous recipe)—which we all have agreed isn't really liver at all....

Millie's Chopped Liver

1 pound chicken livers
Salt and freshly ground
pepper to taste
1 medium onion, finely
chopped

⅓ cup (plus) chicken fat (either
skimmed from the top of
chicken soup or store-bought
—available at kosher meat
markets)
2 hard-boiled eggs

Preheat the broiler part of the oven. Line a heavy-duty baking sheet with either foil or heavy brown paper. If you use brown paper it is important to find some that has not been recycled (as in brown paper bags from the grocery store—recycled paper can be toxic). Dampen the paper lightly with water.

Rinse the livers well and drain them. Blot the excess water with paper towels. Trim off the excess fat. Place the livers on the baking sheets and sprinkle with salt and lots of freshly ground black pepper. Broil for about 5 minutes and then turn the livers over, broiling another 5 minutes. The livers should be dark brown on the outside and still pink inside.

While the livers are cooling, sauté the chopped onion in ⅓ cup of chicken fat and chop the eggs. Chop the livers by hand in a wooden bowl with a hand chopper, if possible—using a food processor makes mush, taking away all the character of chopped liver. Mix in the onions and eggs and additional fat if desired. Add more salt and pepper if necessary.

Serve with a slice of Bermuda onion and a slice of pumpernickel bread or challa, see recipe on page 26.

Serves 8

Pile on the Gelt

I never met a kid who went to Hebrew school by his own free will and choosing. This was something your parents made you do (because their parents made them?). I detested it. Every Sunday morning and Monday and Wednesday afternoon I would be locked up in a cramped, overheated classroom in the basement of our synagogue with forty other bored, fidgety kids who didn't want to be there either listening to Mr. Gittlebaum or Mrs. Cohen blather on for endless hours about some phase of the history of my ancestors. While they tried to pound some knowledge of the Hebrew language into my skull, I was busy daydreaming. I listened to my stomach rumble, bit my nails, drew doodles in my notebook, passed notes, and tuned out. The whole business was a complete waste of time, as far as I was concerned. All this education was really for the boys who would be having their Bar Mitzvahs when they turned thirteen. The girls never got to do anything.

There were one or two things, however, that did capture my interest; I could have listened to the story of Purim over and over again—how the smart, brave, and beautiful Queen Esther saved the Jews from the gallows by foiling the hideous Haman. I liked the singing as well, although Mr. Gittlebaum on the untuned piano doing his Theodore Bikel imitation was far from inspirational.

Chanukah was my least favorite holiday. In our Hebrew school (as well as in our family) we never made a big deal about Chanukah. The adults chanted over and over again that worn-out adage about Chanukah, a minor holiday, not being a substitute for Christmas. Having nagged my parents without success in my very early years, I knew that none of the even most peripheral trappings of the Christian holiday would find themselves into our home. Since my parents weren't gung ho about this minor holiday (our celebration consisted of our going to my aunt's house for potato latkes and us kids lighting the candles for about three nights and then forgetting to do the rest) no one ever gave us presents. It was the worst of both worlds since most of my friends did celebrate Chanukah and everyone else had Christmas. That made me mad, and so every year when Chanukah time rolled around I put extra effort into not paying attention to Mrs. Cohen when she retold the story of Judah and the Maccabees.

One year (I think I was in fourth grade) Mrs. Cohen spent a long Wednesday afternoon going on and on about Chanukah customs; the eight days of candle lighting, the significance of the menorah (the candelabra), the blessings, etc. She started talking about the dreidel (a small top used for a Chanukah game) and I stared very hard out the window, concentrating all my attention on recalling word for word, scene for scene, the last Spin 'N Marty episode on the "Mickey Mouse Club Show"—I recast me as the girl that Spin is madly in love with. There I was riding along on my trusty pony, tossing a lasso, when Mrs. Cohen's voice broke through. She was talking about guilt.

My attention was wrenched back. Guilt—now that's something that could capture the attention of any self-respecting Jew. Mrs. Cohen was saying that the reward for winning at dreidel was guilt—the better you did the more guilt you got—usually from your parents. Now, my parents dished out the guilt if I didn't keep my room neat or forgot to do my homework or was particularly unkind to my brother. While we had never played dreidel at home (I don't think I had ever played it anywhere), I had a difficult time trying to puzzle out why my parents would want to reward this activity with guilt. I spent the rest of the class time ruminating on this puzzle, and then suddenly the answer flashed into my head.

After class I approached Mrs. Cohen to tell her that I had figured out why children get guilt from playing with dreidels. Eyebrows raised in puzzlement she awaited my pronouncement. "Because playing with dreidels is like gambling and the parents don't want the children to grow up to be gamblers, so they give them guilt."

I guess Mrs. Cohen called my parents that afternoon to suggest that they needed to be a little more observant at home, because when I got home from Hebrew school my mother had a big platter of hot, crispy latkes (to go with her famous brisket), the menorah was polished brightly, and two candles stood waiting to be lighted. We said the blessings and then my father pulled a small wooden dreidel out of his pocket. My brother went first, and when the dreidel landed on my letter (indicating that I had won), my father held out a shiny silver dollar. "Here's some gelt for you," he said, smiling. With a flush of embarrassment I realized my mistake, and Dad and I discussed the fact that I should probably pay a little better attention in Hebrew school. I also made it a point to reconsider the merits of this minor holiday—gelt without guilt, what could be bad?

Brisket

5–6 pound brisket
¼ cup water
2 large onions, peeled and sliced
4 stalks celery, cut into ½-inch slices
1 8-ounce bottle chili sauce
4 cloves garlic, peeled and chopped
2 bay leaves

½ cup brown sugar, firmly packed
⅓ cup Dijon mustard
¼ cup red wine vinegar
3 tablespoons molasses
¼ cup soy sauce
1 can beer
½ teaspoon paprika
Salt and pepper to taste
4 potatoes, peeled and sliced

Preheat the oven to 325 degrees with the rack in the lower third, but not bottom, position. Sear the meat, fat side down first, in the bottom of a heavy-duty ovenproof casserole. Turn the meat over and sear the other side. Add to the casserole the water, onions, celery, chili sauce, garlic, bay leaves, brown sugar, mustard, soy sauce, vinegar, and molasses. Cover and cook for 3 hours.

Add the beer, cover and cook 1 more hour, checking occasionally to make sure there is liquid in the pot. Add more water, if necessary. Remove the meat from the pot and pour the sauce into a metal bowl. Discard the bay leaves. Cool broth. Slice the meat when cold. Skim the fat off the sauce, then return the sauce to the casserole or heat-proof serving dish, add the paprika and meat, and reheat on top of the stove, covered. Add salt and pepper to taste.

Parboil the potatoes, then add to the brisket dish to finish cooking.

Serves 8

The Best Brisket Sandwich

The best brisket sandwich is sloppy and a bit of a challenge to eat. Ideally it is made with brisket that has been cooked until it falls apart and is still warm (or reheated for this occasion). You will need thick pieces of bread or a fat, soft roll to absorb the gravy or pan juices.

2 slices of thick, coarse bread like pumpernickel, or an onion or other bulky roll
Dijon mustard
Mayonnaise

Several warm slices of brisket (see preceding recipe)
Pan juices including pieces of onions and carrots

Spread 1 piece of the bread or roll with mustard and the other with mayonnaise. Layer the brisket on 1 piece of bread or roll and add some of the cooked onions and carrots. Spoon on a little of the pan juices and top with the other piece of bread or roll.

You will have to eat this sandwich leaning well over and close to your plate because it should drip—that's part of the fun. Enjoy!

Makes 1 sandwich

Potato Latkes

---

6 Idaho potatoes, peeled   ½ teaspoon baking soda
2 medium onions, diced   1 tablespoon salt
2 extra large eggs   Freshly ground pepper to taste
½ cup flour   Vegetable oil

Grate the potatoes by hand or in a food processor. Cover with cold water and refrigerate for 2–3 hours before starting the latkes. Change the water several times.

Drain off the water and squeeze out any remaining liquid. Mix in the onion. Beat the eggs briefly and then stir them into the potato mixture. Sift together the flour and baking soda and stir into the mixture. Add the salt and pepper.

Pour ¼ inch of oil into a skillet or electric frying pan and heat. When the oil is hot, spoon in mounds of batter to make 2½-inch pancakes. Brown very well on both sides. Replenish oil as necessary, waiting to make sure the oil is hot before proceeding.

Serve the latkes hot with sour cream or applesauce (see page 90). The latkes can be frozen after they have completely cooled. Store them in heavy-duty zip-lock freezer bags and heat in a 400-degree oven.

Makes 3–4 dozen latkes

Baked Potatoes

The house in which I grew up was on the border of Hartford and a then-undeveloped rural town called Bloomfield. Down the block and across the street was the end of civilization—an area we kids referred to as "the tracks." It was several acres of fields and woods bounded on one side by a long row of postwar cheese-box houses, on two sides by housing projects, and on the fourth side by a swamp. A set of railroad tracks separated the meadow from the woods and a puny stream trickled into the swamp, creating a haven for mosquitoes in the summer and a place to ice-skate in the winter. These days any parent in their right mind would never consider letting their grade-school children go off and play for hours in the setting I have just described. But these were *those* days, and the woods were safe and full of adventures waiting to happen.

Oh, those days when the snow was higher and whipped by bone-chilling winds into magnificently high drifts that set the stage for king-of-the-mountain shoving matches and perfect snow angels, the winters when the mercury dipped down below zero and stayed there for days on end and the swamp in our woods froze into black ice. Every day after school, dressed in layers of itchy woolen long johns, equally itchy woolen pants, coats, hats, scarves, and mittens, we would hitch our skates over our shoulders and head out into the fading afternoon light.

My across-the-street neighbor, Arthur Kelly, was by virtue of his size and strength of his opinions our self-proclaimed leader. A.J. (Arthur, Junior) was the one who got to test the ice, who got to be the kingpin in crack-the-whip, and who got to say if it was warm enough for all the other kids to skate without their coats, scarves, etc., without catching pneumonia (as long as we promised not to tell our parents we were acting on his advice in case we did catch pneumonia). He also got to direct all the other kids in the tedious job of shoveling the snow off our pond. The rest of the gang was made up of A.J.'s assorted brothers and sisters and my best friend, Susan.

The frozen meadow ground didn't give an inch under our flapping galoshes. The field grass and low bushes that scratched our legs and deposited burrs on our shorts in summer now broke in brittle pieces as we plowed through swinging our skates in wide and potentially dangerous arcs.

We always looked carefully as we crossed the tracks, even though none of us had ever seen a train there. I remember consciously not asking my parents if those tracks were abandoned—I wanted to believe they were used—even if it happened when I wasn't around. We once left some pennies on the rails as a test to see if the next day we would find them flattened and distorted. The next day they were gone.

Once we crossed the tracks the woods closed in and the daylight diffused into dusk. We quickly shoveled off any snow that accumulated the night before and sat down on the rough wooden bench we had fashioned out of a plank and some big rocks and put on our skates. A.J. started a fire using purloined matches from his mother's cigarette case and odd pieces of wood.

While there were some smooth places, much of the surface of the pond (which, if you recall, was called the "swamp" in warmer weather) was punctuated by roots, rocks, twigs, and crusts of unshoveled snow. The challenge to the skater was not so much staying upright but staying upright and avoiding the debris. Crack-the-whip took on a really scary (and dangerous) edge as those of us on the end (I was always on the end) held on for dear life as we were propelled around the ice at breakneck (an apt description) speed. Invariably my nose got smashed against a tree trunk or my ankle was wrenched as the blade of my skate caught on a partially submerged root, but I wasted little time with tears (since the kids never got concerned unless you knocked yourself out), picked myself up, wiped my bloodied nose with a partially frozen mitten, and skated like mad to catch up to the suicide line.

One of the scariest and (of course) most exhilarating challenges was to walk several yards upstream on the brook, the upper layer of which was frozen solid, and skate down. One usually did this in a tuck position so that (1) you could see impending doom (rocks, frozen leaves embedded in the ice, thin spots) in the deepening twilight and (2) so that you had a shorter distance to fall once you encountered one of the aforementioned obstacles. It was necessary to give out a Comanche war cry as you executed this insane stunt.

A.J.'s fires were always pyrotechnic masterpieces. He had the kids scrambling on wobbly skates through the woods to bring him (usually soggy) logs that would alternately smoke furiously and then send showers of tiny sparks into the early evening sky. Our hands were sticky and sweet smelling from pitch as we dutifully brought burnable offerings and then stood as close as we dared while the heat of the fire made our soggy woolen coats steam and smell like a pack of large, wet dogs.

A.J. poked and prodded and added branches to his fire until he was satisfied with it and then reached into his coat pocket and brought forth six good-sized potatoes wrapped in foil. These he carefully deposited near the center of the inferno. Knowing we had a good half hour before we could eat them, and feeling our faces beginning to blister from the heat, we returned to skating. A.J., guarding his position as chief pyro man, remained by the fire, prodding and poking the potatoes as if this would make them cook faster; instead, all he managed to do was shred the foil.

Tired of getting my nose bashed and feeling the lumps rising on my shins, I left the others playing crack-the-whip and would skate by myself to explore the boundaries of the swamp. I made sure to look for the first star so I could make a wish—

Star light, star bright,
First star I see tonight,
Wish I may, wish I might,
Have this wish come true tonight.

My friends' voices faded behind as I made my way carefully through the trees. All I heard was the sound of my skates and the rustle of stubborn oak leaves who foolishly thought that if they clung all winter to the black silhouetted branches they would be rejuvenated come spring. In that magic place under the deepening winter sky I was the child in *The Snow Queen*, my vision distorted by the magic glass; I was Sargent Preston's first girl assistant; I was Sonja Henie practicing on her private ice pond. Sonja Henie was practicing her famous spiral position. She picked up speed, flung her arms open, gracefully lifted her leg up behind her higher and higher, her back arched, head held high, until she was gliding in perfect poise before the stunned audience. Sonja moved into a spin and promptly tripped over a rock. As I sat on the ice rubbing yet another bruise, I heard A.J.'s voice calling through the woods that the potatoes were ready and was happy to leave Sonja behind to practice her spins unobserved.

Getting the potatoes out of the fire was not nearly as easy as getting them in. A lot of maneuvering with sticks and swearing on A.J.'s part was bolstered by a lot of shouted advice from us kids. The potatoes were alternately stabbed, rolled, and bashed into submission and out of the fire. The heavenly smell filled the air. It was the substantially comforting, familiar smell of something good to eat that would satisfy and fill up your empty stomach. It smelled like Mom's kitchen had suddenly been transported to the woods; it was a smell connected to love and nurturing. The kids wasted no time grabbing for them. The first thing to do once you picked up a hot potato was to hold it in your mittened hand for as long as you could before the heat became unbearable, then you transferred it to your other hand and/or tossed it up in the air until it cooled down a bit. The next step was to peel the remaining tinfoil away and brush away any visible dirt (you may ask just how much dirt a hungry ten-year-old can see in the middle of the woods in the evening). We sat on the bench huddled close together, our skates loosened, the first painful tingles reminding us that our toes had been jammed together for too long, nibbling at the delicious warmth cradled in our hands. I savored the nutty taste, the mild bitterness, and papery texture of the blackened skin (I loved the burnt parts and still do). Pinching the ends forced an explosion of irresistible steaming whiteness that burned my mouth and sent scalding waves down my throat, finally heating my stomach.

Long before the feeling returned to my toes, all that was left of my potato was a memory of white crumbs clinging to my mittens. The moonlight made wavy neon lines in the pond's irregular surface, the sky was the deep purple of the song, and it was time to head for home. We kicked over the fire, hid our shovel behind a tree, and struggled with skates that surely weighed more now than when we first made our way here.

The tracks seemed ominous and we crossed quickly, peering over our shoulders for hoboes that someone's father had told them lurked in the woods. Hadn't they snitched our flattened pennies?

"First lights!" yelled A.J.'s little sister as we emerged from the meadow and got a glimpse of streetlights and civilization.

The call of "last one home's a rotten egg," sent a final wave of energy through us that sped us on to the welcome lights of our warm homes where dinner was waiting.

Potato Skins with Baked Eggs

The next best thing to those camp-fire baked potatoes is this dish, which actually can be cooked in a covered barbeque grill.

4 large Idaho potatoes	4 extra large eggs
4 tablespoons butter	1 cup shredded Monterey Jack
Salt, freshly ground black	cheese
pepper, and cayenne to taste	

Preheat the oven to 400 degrees (or fire up a gas or charcoal grill) and bake the potatoes for 1 hour, or until done. If using the grill it is preferable to wrap the potatoes in foil. Cool slightly, cut them in half lengthwise, and place the halves on a baking sheet cut sides up. Set the broiler on high with the rack ⅓ down from the top.

Scoop out at least half the meat from the potato and mash it with the butter. Add salt and pepper and a dash of cayenne to taste. Replace the mashed potato back in the potato skin, patting it down well to make room for the egg.

Carefully, so as not to disturb the yolk, break an egg into each potato half. Sprinkle very generously with the shredded cheese and broil (or place back in the grill and lower the top) for approximately 2–3 minutes (longer for the grill) until the egg is set and the cheese completely melted. Keep a careful eye on the potatoes while they are cooking—if the cheese browns too much before the egg is cooked, move the baking sheet to a lower position. Serve immediately.

Serves 4

Casseroles—or
What Are You Trying to Hide?

I got a headache whenever my mother's deep oval Pyrex baking dish made its appearance on the straw hot plate in the middle of the kitchen table. Sometimes I got a stomachache and a coughing fit and double vision as well. I could have easily worked up to cardiac arrest except my mother, fully anticipating my reaction, cut short the melodrama employing that ageless noogie of the psyche—guilt.

"I've been on my feet all day making this dinner and this is what I get from you? There are children starving in Korea (we had run out of Chinese children to feed?) and you act like this." To whom would I have been reported? Eleanor Roosevelt? Pearl S. Buck?

Now that I have tried to palm casseroles off on my children, I know that unless Mom was opening the assorted cans of ingredients with her fingernails and a nail file, there was no way that she was on her feet for more than twenty minutes whipping that dish together.

The thing that created the casserole anxiety was the fact that I wasn't able to see exactly what it was that I was going to have to stick in my mouth, chew, and ultimately swallow. I needed food to be instantly identifiable; roast beef always looking like a thin, flat, oval slice of dark brown with no visible fat and *of course* no blood; scrambled eggs—fluffy yellow with no black pepper or overcooked (brown, crusty) parts and certainly no added ingredients like onion, herbs, or cottage cheese; tapioca pudding—light yellow, lumpy congealed glop with no hidden fruit lurking beneath the surface. Like most children I liked things plain, not mixed with cream sauce, blended with last night's vegetables, and topped with any of the following: crushed Ritz crackers, crushed cornflakes, crushed potato chips, or toasted buttered bread crumbs. To my mind that was a way of taking good food (I'm talking about the toppings, not the leftover vegetables or cream sauce) and making it perfectly repulsive.

I automatically labeled as ''casserole'' any dish in which:

1. *Food left over from a previous meal had been chopped, ground up, crumbled, or pureed.*
2. *Anything from the above category had been combined with small pieces of cut-up vegetables.*
3. *Anything from the above categories had been mixed with a cream sauce or the contents of a can of any of Campbell's creamed soups.*
4. *All or any of the above had been sprinkled with an aforementioned crumb topping.*
5. *Anything served in my mother's oval Pyrex casserole dish.*

My deep-seated casserole dislike stemmed from a single, well-documented incident that was discovered during my long psychoanalysis: my mother (a truly marvelous cook who, if I am to be completely honest, rarely fell back on casseroles) was once perversely influenced by a flashy cover of *Ladies' Home Journal* that promised to let her feed her family delicious, nutritious, and attractive meals for Virtually Pennies a Serving and in a Matter of Seconds!!!!!! and threw judgment to the winds and violated my number-one rule of food: *Never mix tuna fish with anything other than Hellmann's mayonnaise and a little bit of chopped celery.*

While under the twisted, sinister influence of this Article from Hell she mixed together several cans of white meat tuna, several cans of assorted Chinese vegetables, a generous dash of soy sauce, and one can of cream of celery soup. The top was sprinkled with broken-up Chinese noodles—so we could tell the dish was Chinese in theme—and served over rice.

''Chicken chow mein,'' announced Mom proudly as she set the oval casserole upon the straw hot plate. I don't remember her looking shifty eyed at me to see my reaction, but I'm sure she must have.

The steam poured forth as she set about scooping it onto our plates and I had to admit that, for a casserole, it actually smelled pretty good. I started to mention that I had a migraine coming on but thought the better of it when I tasted the concoction and thought that I could get most of it down. I remember thinking that the chicken wasn't exactly chicken-like but couldn't quite put my finger on what was unusual. After all, it looked like chicken and with all that stuff covering it, Frank Perdue would have been hard-pressed to tell the difference.

It wasn't until after dinner when I was scraping the dishes into the garbage and I came upon the tuna cans in the trash that the awful truth hit. I was repulsed. I was furious. I got hysterical. My beloved and sacred food had been desecrated, defiled—by my own mother who should have not only known better but should have thought ahead to the hell I would raise if I ever found out the awful truth.

That was it. From that day casseroles were right down there with broiled calf's liver and boiled tongue. I would not be budged into trying even the tiniest bit. When the Pyrex oval showed up on the table I made myself peanut butter and jelly and vowed that I would never ever make my children eat casseroles.

Vows like that are made to be broken. While I managed to studiously avoid casserole-type dishes throughout the rest of my childhood, it was during my late teens (remember the experimental years?) that I gave it another try. During college I went home for the weekend with my friend Polly who lived in Vermont. She was a hearty, athletic outdoorsy kind of girl who had been telling me about the joys of a Vermont winter—skiing, skating, tobogganing. Having grown up in New England and having been of the opinion that winter was something you suffered through until spring came and made the frozen months a nasty memory, I was ready to be enlightened; I wanted to learn to enjoy winter.

Her home was far up north, near the Canadian border, a tiny town of green-shuttered white farmhouses, a village green (really a village white in this weather), and acres of rolling fields hedged by formidable mountains that were criss-crossed with ski trails. After a warm welcome from Polly's parents and a fast sandwich, we raced to throw on several layers of warm clothing and went outside to help Polly's younger brothers build a snow fort. For over an hour we rolled the heavy snow into giant balls and hauled it over to a pile that soon grew monstrous in size. We tunneled in and around it (meanwhile dodging snowballs from the kids who, crazed with happiness to have their sister home again, cavorted like two puppies in the drifts in between potshots at us). We sprayed the final edifice with water so that it would freeze solid and stay put at least until late April. Then it was on to the barn to collect cross-country skis. Polly showed me how to strap on the skis and we were off.

Shuss, shuss, shuss. We fell into the rhythm, and our skis made soft, regular noises as we crossed the wide meadow and headed toward a stand of trees. The powder thrown up by our skis flashed in the sunlight; the sky, so brightly blue it dazzled this city girl, framed whisps of high clouds strung along the mountain peaks. The air was so cold and pure I felt like I was inhaling menthol. My lungs screamed with the unexpected demands of physical labor, my thighs balked at the slight rise ahead. But I pushed on, arms accustomed only to carrying a stack of schoolbooks now pushing my weight with the ski poles, following Polly's distant form, not wanting to be left behind but wobbly with the effort and drunk with the thrill of exertion.

It was slower going in the woods as the trail had not been broken. We saw blue jays fighting over territory and squirrels chattered at us for disturbing their privacy. I wanted to stop and take off my jacket, scarf, and hat. I was dripping with the effort of keeping up with Polly, and I was beginning to hear serious complaints from my empty stomach. Several miles into the woods Polly, finally heeding the cry of her empty stomach, decided that it was time to turn around. It was slower going on the way home simply because both of us had run out of steam. I was hallucinating about one-pound steaks and French fries. I thought about onion soup with melted cheese on top with such concentration that I swear I could smell it. Polly made this reverie worse by rhapsodizing about her mother's famous apple strudel. Just thinking about it made my knees weak, and I promptly crossed my skis and became one with the ground. I lay on my back, too weary to untangle my encumbered limbs, looking up at the impossibly blue sky bisected by bushy pine boughs. Polly had skied on ahead, so the only noise I could hear was my labored breathing and the occasional plop of melting snow falling from the trees. Every other sound and movement was muffled by the snow. It was so peaceful in the woods. I screwed my eyes almost shut so that the trees receded and that deep blueness became the still, warm waters of the Caribbean. Whispered breaths of winter wind became the gentle sound of crystal clear water lapping fine pink sand. I closed my eyes and waited for a native in a gaudy tropical shirt to bring me a piña colada garnished with a hibiscus blossom.

As the snow began to permeate the seat of my pants, my mental stereoscope shifted to the headline "City girl succumbs to hunger while skiing." This was also a good fantasy because I could then imagine what the brave forest rangers got to eat after they found my frozen corpse. I was in the middle of picking out my postfuneral buffet when Polly's voice rang through the woods warning me in no uncertain terms that I was going to miss supper if I didn't shake a leg. Dying in the woods suddenly didn't seem so romantic. Dead people didn't get to eat apple strudel and French fries. Those last miles were endless, my legs fueled only by the thought of what Polly's mother was going to feed us. I whooped with joy at the sight of the white farmhouse with the thin stream of smoke rising from its chimney.

I was amazed at the effort required to get my legs to haul me upstairs and how every muscle complained as I bent to peel off my soaked layers. Polly directed me to soak my bones in the old-fashioned claw-footed bathtub, and I was delighted to obey. Incredible cooking smells danced from the kitchen, up the stairs, and wafted under the bathroom door. Butter sizzling, onions browning, a hint of garlic, the intoxicating aroma of fresh-baked bread. Already weak from exertion and faint with hunger I wondered how I could make it down the stairs. From the bathroom window I could see our snow fort gleaming in the moonlight like a white marble abstract sculpture out on the middle of the front lawn. My chest swelled with pride at the accomplishment that made my back ache with the agony of the effort.

Dressed in a warm flannel shirt and dry jeans I tentatively navigated my way down the stairs and followed my nose into the kitchen. A tray of cookies, fresh from the oven, sat on the back of the wood stove in the center of the kitchen. The wooden table flanked by two benches was set with pottery plates and red-fringed, handwoven napkins. A crock in the center of the table held assorted spoons, knives, and forks. Polly's mom poured us a mug of steaming cocoa that disappeared instantly, taking some of the edge off my ravenous hunger. The boys giggled and poked each other, arguing about who had the bigger chocolate mustache. Polly's mom bent over the oven, two heavy mitts on her hands, and pulled out a very large version of my mother's deep oval Pyrex casserole dish.

Now, to be perfectly honest, my heart only stopped for a second, my disappointment was dramatically tempered by my need for nourishment. At this point I would have happily consumed the better part of the *New York Times*'s Sunday edition raw or boiled. Obviously, a casserole was not what I had been fantasizing about—but it was hot and it was food and I was starving. At first glance it didn't look too much like the casseroles I was used to. Instead of crunched-up stuff on top there were small round biscuits placed right next to each other covering the entire top. The inside had begun to bubble over the top forming a glaze. Polly's mom ladeled out heaping servings to us, and without preamble we dug in. The biscuits were ethereally tender and flaky, practically melting in my mouth, leaving behind a buttery memory. The pieces of pink salmon were large enough to be easily identified and were cooked to savory perfection. Tiny pearl onions (I didn't know I loved pearl onions) and bright green peas added a little crunch to each forkful. The sauce was more like a gravy in that it had a personality all its own—rich and golden in color and silken in texture with the amber taste of sherry giving it depth and distinction. I had three helpings before I came up for air and remembered my manners, telling Polly's mother how wonderful her casserole was.

"Well, we don't call it casserole, honey," she said in her twangy up-New England accent. "We call it salmon pie and I'm glad you like it."

In my bed much later that night, well fortified by three pieces of apple strudel and more than enough peanut butter cookies, I lay under a warm down comforter, assessing my aches and pains and wondered, as I drifted off to sleep, if I could have some of that salmon pie for breakfast.

Salmon Pie

---

1 cup fish stock, either homemade, commercially prepared, or made by dissolving ½ cube Knorr's fish bouillon in 1 cup boiling water; *or* one cup vegetable broth
1 cup dry white wine
6 tablespoons butter, softened
1 medium onion, minced
2 cloves garlic, minced
6 tablespoons flour
2½ cups light cream
1 teaspoon thyme
Pinch of saffron (2 to 3 threads)
2 teaspoons Dijon mustard
salt and white pepper to taste
1 cup pearl onions, fresh or frozen (not defrosted)
1½ cups peas, fresh or frozen
2 cups mushrooms, sliced
1 medium red pepper, chopped
2 1-pound cans salmon, drained, picked over to remove the bones and skin, or 1¾ pounds fresh cooked salmon fillet, skinned and cut into 1-inch cubes

Combine the fish stock or vegetable broth and wine and bring to a simmer. Meanwhile, melt the butter in a large skillet and briefly sauté the onion and garlic, just until transparent. Whisk in the flour and cook over moderate heat for five minutes, stirring constantly.

Add the hot stock, beating with a wire whisk until there are no lumps of flour visible. Continue to stir until the mixture begins to simmer. Whisk in the cream. Lower the heat and simmer for an additional five minutes. Add the thyme, saffron, mustard, and salt and pepper to taste.

In a large bowl combine the pearl onions, peas, and red pepper. Stir in the sauce and then very gently, so as not to break up the pieces too much, fold in the salmon. Place the mixture in a buttered ovenproof casserole and top with the following biscuits.

FOR THE BISCUITS

2 cups flour, measured after sifting
½ teaspoon salt
1 teaspoon baking powder
½ teaspoon baking soda
⅓ cup solid vegetable shortening (such as Crisco)
¾ cup buttermilk

Sift the dry ingredients together. Cut in the shortening until the mixture resembles coarse meal. Dribble in the buttermilk, stirring with a fork until a soft dough forms. Turn onto a lightly floured board and knead fifteen or so times. Pat out to a 9-inch circle and, using a floured cookie cutter or drinking glass, cut into 2-inch circles.

Preheat the oven to 425 degrees with the rack in the center position. Cover the top of the salmon mixture with the biscuits. The biscuits should be touching. Bake for 10 minutes at 425 degrees and then lower the oven temperature to 350 degrees and bake an additional 30 minutes. If the biscuits start to get too brown cover the casserole loosely with foil.

Serves 8

Apple Strudel

FOR THE FILLING

5 Cortland or McIntosh apples   ½ cup golden raisins
1 cup granulated sugar   ½ cup walnuts, chopped
1 teaspoon cinnamon   2 tablespoons sweet butter,
2 tablespoons flour   cut into small pieces
2 tablespoons instant tapioca

Peel and cut the apples into small cubed pieces. Mix the sugar and cinnamon and toss with the apples. Mix in the flour, tapioca, raisins, and walnuts. Mix in the sweet butter. Set aside while you prepare the pastry.

FOR THE PASTRY

½ pound sweet butter   ½ cup plain dry bread crumbs
1 package phyllo dough (available
   in the freezer section of supermarkets or in specialty
   food stores)

Melt the butter in a small saucepan and scrape off as much of the white foam (milk solids) that rise to the top as possible. This will keep the butter from burning.

Remove the dough from the package and unroll it so that it sits vertically on your work space. Cover the dough with plastic wrap or a very lightly dampened cloth. Remove 1 sheet of dough (keep the others covered so they won't dry out) and place it on a plastic-wrap-lined baking sheet. Brush the entire sheet with butter. Place another sheet of dough on top and brush with butter. Repeat 2 more times until you have 4 sheets. Butter the fourth sheet and then sprinkle with the bread crumbs. Continue stacking and buttering the sheets until you have 7 in all.

Spoon the filling along the bottom edge of the dough leaving a 1½-inch border along the bottom and a 1-inch border at the ends. Dot the filling with the butter. Flip the border over the filling and continue to roll the pastry away from you, ending with the seam side down. Use the plastic wrap under the dough to help in the rolling.

The strudel can be frozen at this point—wrap it completely in the plastic wrap and then in a layer of foil—or it can be baked.

TO BAKE THE STRUDEL

3 tablespoons butter, melted
1 tablespoon sugar mixed with
1 teaspoon cinnamon

Preheat the oven to 350 degrees with the rack in the center position. Line a heavy-duty, rimmed baking sheet with foil and butter the foil. Place the strudel on the prepared baking sheet, brush it liberally with butter, and sprinkle with the cinnamon sugar. Bake 45 minutes or until the pastry is lightly browned. Serve hot.

Serves 8

Good-bye

Was it by law or tradition that Jewish children weren't taken to funerals? I can only speak for my house where no child was even told of a death until months later, when one of us would innocently ask where Uncle Saul or Aunt Sofie was and have to face a wall of embarrassed silence until one of the adults, after considerable hemming and hawing, would take us into another room and manage to blurt out the truth. "We only wanted to spare you the sadness," was the excuse, but we knew it was their difficulty in dealing with death that left them hanging and us uninformed.

I never knew about funerals when I was a small child. I thought that when someone died there was a party to which everyone brought food. This was a reaction to death I never questioned as a youngster, but upon reflection I suppose the antidote of food for the pain of loss is a natural one. It is soothing when you are ragged, it is (hopefully and in our family predictably) uplifting when you are depleted, and it gives everyone something to talk about as well as creating endless distraction in its preparation and serving. Given the way death was never actually talked about in our family, I think it was only natural that the main activity centered around something that was meant to go in your mouth so that you *couldn't* talk.

In the house the mirrors were covered with cloths or scarves (or in some cases they were turned to the wall), bridge chairs were set up in rows in the parlor or living room, and a pitcher of water and a hand towel were placed on the stoop outside the front door. The party was called sitting shivah and it went on for a week, which meant at any given time of the day people would show up at your door (bearing pastry, noodle puddings, tuna casseroles, and the like), say a prayer while rinsing their hands with water from the pitcher, exchange hugs and deep sighs with the black-clad grown-ups inside, give their heavy damp fur coats and scarves to the maid hired for the occasion, and put their food in the kitchen.

The kitchen would be full of women—mothers, grandmothers, aunts, sisters, grown-up girl cousins—in their stocking feet (I thought this was a religious custom until I started wearing high heels), red-eyed, with wadded-up damp Kleenexes stuffed into their cuffs or bosoms, shooing out children underfoot, arranging food: putting cookies on plates, cutting poppy seed cake in thick wedges, spooning mounds of potato and salmon salads onto beds of lettuce covering the large, gold-rimmed china plate someone found stuck behind a pile of everyday dishes. They unwrapped foil-covered packages of roast turkey, combined it with Tupperware trays of boiled chicken, rewrapped the overflow of Jell-O mold and pickled herring in plastic containers all the while bemoaning the lack of space in the bursting refrigerator. They made artful platters of bagels and lox (served with slices of Bermuda onion and both plain and chive cream cheese), stacked cubes of honey cake, jelly roll, kuchen, and marble cake, and cut gefilte fish into bite-sized pieces that could be skewered with a colored toothpick before dipping it in horseradish on the way to your mouth. If you were lucky there was a bowl of homemade chopped chicken liver ready to be spread on Ritz crackers with one of those funny little curved spreaders with a tiny china handle. Add to this platters of sliced tomatoes, cucumbers, celery sticks, and dill pickles, baskets of sliced pumpernickel, sissle rye, corn rye, and marble bread and you begin to have an idea of the bounty of the shivah table. Bear in mind that as people filled their plates and ate, the doorbell rang and more dishes were deposited in the kitchen, so the selection on the table changed steadily.

As Cousin Bert polished off the last of the stuffed cabbage, the platter was instantly replaced by the crew of ladies from the kitchen who shuffled back and forth on stocking feet bearing empty platters from the table and full ones from the kitchen. Desserts were all mixed up with salads and cold meats; the eating went on all day and night, sometimes started with a bite of cake, chased by a bit of herring, then a nibble of coconut macaroon, and then half a bagel. Three or four courses piled up on paper plates; combinations of food that one never thought about before turned out to be simply delicious, like apricot Jell-O mold and a slice of kosher bologna.

The centerpiece of the table was always the same: a large bowl of shelled hard-boiled eggs. The eggs were symbolic and everyone had their own version of what the symbolism was, from the egg representing the life cycle, to the great theory I heard as an adult: the egg is the ultimate symbol of cholesterol—it's a reminder of what probably killed the person we were mourning. No one ever ate the eggs, and since there was a never-ending procession of them making their way through the front door, they did time on the table for one day and then ended up in the form of egg salad next to the boiled chicken the next day.

On the sideboard flickering in memoriam were Yortzeit candles in extra-tall glasses. Their weak light behind the Hebrew- and English-printed labels glanced off bottles of schnapps, seltzer, and cream soda, and the nearby mismatched assortment of kitchen glasses that stood ready for the pouring.

The children, somehow always unsure of what was really going on and therefore uncomfortable and on edge, raced through the house, stopping briefly in the kitchen to grab a piece of mandl-broyt and a glass of soda, until an adult grabbed the ringleader firmly by the upper arm and suggested that they all go upstairs for a quiet game of Monopoly. The little kids were confused by the lack of concrete information and adult supervision; unless (God forbid) it was your parent or sibling that had died, no one had bothered to explain that old Uncle Hyman (who had been in a nursing home for the past ten months) had finally succumbed at age ninety-seven and this resulting week of shivah was in his memory.

In a downstairs bedroom or den the rabbi would consult with the immediate family, and every once in a while he would come into the living room to lead the skullcapped men, their shoulders draped in prayer shawls, in prayer delivered in a fast and mournful singsong Hebrew the words of which I didn't understand but the melody I knew by heart. I would lean in the kitchen doorway watching my father, my uncles, and my post-Bar Mitzvah boy cousins rocking gently back and forth chanting the Kaddish feeling a mixture of jealousy and awe—these males were clearly privy to the secret ceremonies and deeper meanings of the goings-on, and the inherent message was that while the men's place was in the living room (just like their place in shul was downstairs where the action was), the women belonged in the kitchen.

Later that night after the waves of mourners had subsided, the extended family sat around in the living room, women with their swollen, stocking feet resting on footstools, the men cradling small glasses of schnapps. Each close relative wore a small black arm band or black button with a piece of ripped black cloth attached to it on their lapel. This symbolized the rending of your clothing in sorrow.

The women had had it with the kitchen for a while; consequently several heavy crystal ashtrays threatened to overflow with the afternoon's debris, and shaky piles of paper plates accumulated on the coffee table accompanied by crumpled napkins and half-drunk glasses of soda. Most of the kids had departed, leaving the others sulking and whining (no television during the week of shivah) or just plain exhausted to the point of tears.

The adults would quietly and with hushed reverence begin to tell stories about Uncle Hy or Grandma Flo or whomever it was that the family was celebrating the memory of. As the bottle of schnapps was emptied and the smell of Uncle Max's cigar smoke drifted across the room, turning the air hazy and dreamily brown-blue, the stories grew livelier and the voices in fact became raucous. These poor old dead people were brought alive, made young again by the touching and often hilarious stories the family recounted. Tales of tipsy indiscretions, honeymoon escapades, ridiculous sibling battles rose to the top of the family's mind and fell off their tongues like bubbles flowing to the top of a glass of seltzer. Tears of laughter streamed down cheeks where hours before dripped tears of sorrow. This strange behavior caught the children's attention and broke the spell of gloom that had trickled down upon them; now sad, now happy, victims of the adults' taboos of speaking to them about death.

Midnight found most of the family held suspended in exhausted, dreamless sleep. You might find Grandpa Abe or old Uncle Lou still sitting in the living room, each one quietly contemplating their own send-off, and you might find Grandma Bea and Aunt Frieda drying the last of the coffee cups, putting off the moment when they had to find room in the fridge for yet another bowl of hard-cooked eggs, wipe down the counter yet one more time, turn out the lights, and go to bed, leaving the Yortzeit candles flickering all alone in the dark.

My Egg Salad

There is egg salad and there is egg salad. The stuff that has sat all day in a refrigerated deli case is not even worth considering. Homemade is best and here's how to do it right.

6 fresh eggs	Dash of Tabasco
½–⅔ cup Hellmann's mayonnaise	Salt to taste
2–3 tablespoons Dijon mustard	Lots of freshly ground pepper

Place the eggs in a medium-sized pan and cover with cold water. Add a tablespoon of salt—this supposedly keeps the eggs from cracking during cooking. Bring the water slowly to a simmer and continue to simmer for 15 minutes. Immediately rinse the eggs with cold water and crack off the shells. Use 2 knives in a crisscross cutting motion to mash the eggs, adding the mayonnaise, mustard, Tabasco, and salt and pepper. Serve while still warm, if possible, on fresh challa or pumpernickel bread. A half-sour pickle and handfuls of Wise's potato chips and you're all set. That's egg salad.

Serves 4–6

Salmon Salad

1 1-pound can salmon
  (I prefer Bumblebee)
2 hard-boiled eggs
1 small Bermuda onion,
  minced

2–3 tablespoons mayonnaise
  (I prefer Hellmann's)
Lemon juice and freshly
  ground black pepper to taste

Drain the salmon and discard the juice as well as any visible bones. Chop the eggs coarsely. Mix the salmon, eggs, and onion together and then mix in as much mayonnaise as desired. Season with lemon juice and pepper.

Serves 4

Noodle Pudding I

1 pound wide egg noodles
4 eggs, separated
½ cup sugar
2 teaspoons baking powder
½ cup sour cream
1 cup cottage cheese

½ cup apricot preserves
1 teaspoon vanilla
1 stick (4 ounces) sweet
  (unsalted) butter, melted
1 cup golden raisins

Preheat the oven to 350 degrees with the rack in the center position. Butter generously a 10 × 13-inch ovenproof rectangular casserole. Boil the noodles until they are al dente, rinse with cold water, and set aside.

Beat the egg yolks and sugar until the mixture is thick and pale yellow in color. Add in the baking powder, taking care that it is mixed in well. Mix in the sour cream, cottage cheese, preserves, and vanilla. Stir in the melted butter.

Whip the egg whites until they are firm but not stiff and fold them into the other mixture. Fold together the egg mixture, the noodles, and the raisins. Place in prepared pan and bake for 1 hour or until the top is golden.

Serves 10

Noodle Pudding II

This is a much richer, sweeter noodle pudding than the one on the previous page. It makes an excellent brunch dish and is equally wonderful eaten cold the next day.

1 pound ¼-inch egg noodles
6 eggs, lightly beaten
¼ cup sugar
6 tablespoons butter, melted
1 cup sour cream
1 pound cottage cheese
½ pound (8 ounces) farmer's cheese, or whole milk ricotta
¼ pound (4 ounces) cream cheese at room temperature
2 cups whole milk

Preheat the oven to 350 degrees with the rack in the center position. Butter an 11 × 13-inch (larger is o.k., smaller will be too small) rectangular Pyrex dish or an ovenproof casserole. Cook the noodles in boiling water al dente. Drain and place in prepared dish. Combine all the other ingredients and pour evenly over the noodles. Bake for 30 minutes. Meanwhile prepare the following topping.

FOR THE TOPPING

⅔ cup sliced almonds, crushed, but not finely ground
2 tablespoons melted butter
4 tablespoons brown sugar
1 cup apricot preserves

Combine all the ingredients in a small saucepan and stir over medium heat until softened and well combined. Drop by spoonfuls over the noodles and spread evenly. Return to the 350-degree oven for 50 minutes to 1 hour or until the top is browned and bubbly. Serve warm.

Serves 12–16

Apricot Jell-O Mold

This recipe will serve up to 16 people and can be used as a side dish at brunch or lunch, with noodle pudding or potato kugel, blintzes, or bagels and lox. My children have been known to eat it for breakfast, lunch, dinner, and as a midnight snack. It is best to make it at least the day before and can be made up to as many as 2 days before you plan to serve it.

I have had some difficulty at times locating apricot Jell-O. When I can't find it I use peach Jell-O (which is, for some strange reason, easier to locate—although I can't imagine why). You might want to experiment with your own versions. A combination of peach and raspberry Jell-O is great, although I find orange Jell-O turns out to be much too sweet for my taste.

This dish can be served unmolded—that's the hard way—or from a tall glass bowl (footed is nice, if you don't have one, don't worry). If you are neat, the layers look really pretty and no one will even notice that you didn't unmold it.

8 cups apricot nectar	2 large cans unpeeled apricot
1 cup water	halves
2 large packages of apricot Jell-O	1 8-ounce package cream cheese
1 small package apricot Jell-O	1 pint sour cream

Pour the nectar and the water into a large pan and sprinkle the Jell-O on top. Gently heat the mixture, stirring constantly until all the Jell-O is melted. Be very careful not to get the mixture hot enough to simmer or boil. When the Jell-O is completely dissolved, transfer the mixture to another bowl to help cool it down. Refrigerate the Jell-O while you prepare the apricots.

Drain the apricot halves well, discarding the syrup. Use a teaspoon to scoop out a ball of cream cheese slightly smaller than a walnut. Use your fingers to form this into a ball and place it in the hollow of one of the apricot halves. Place the other half over it to make a sandwich with the cream cheese in the center. Do this with all the apricot halves and set them aside.

If you are going to unmold the Jell-O mold, rinse a 12-cup metal or plastic mold with water and tap it upside down to remove most of the water. Use a large ladle to place some of the

Jell-O mixture to the depth of about 1 inch in the bottom of the mold. Refrigerate. If you use a glass bowl (one that holds at least 12 cups), don't rinse it with water. Ladle enough Jell-O mixture to cover the entire bottom to the depth of about 1 inch.

When the Jell-O is semifirm (you can still make a dent in it with your finger), place the apricots on top. They might slide around—don't worry. Ladle more Jell-O on top to almost cover the apricots. An easy way to do this—if you have enough room, is to keep the bowl or mold in the refrigerator and ladle in the liquid Jell-O without moving the bowl or mold.

When that layer is almost set, add another inch or so of Jell-O and allow it to set until completely firm. By now you should have used ⅔ of the Jell-O.

Mix the sour cream to soften and then carefully spread it on top of the firm Jell-O. Wipe the sides of the bowl with a damp paper towel if you happened to smudge any sour cream. Very carefully spread a thin layer of Jell-O on top of the sour cream. Chill until firm, then add the rest of the Jell-O.

If, while you are waiting for a layer to get firm, your liquid Jell-O starts to set up, transfer it back to the pan and very gently heat it, stirring constantly until it is liquid again.

If you have used a mold, wait until just before serving to un-mold. Have ready a flat platter slightly larger than your mold. Also have a towel spread out on the counter next to the sink. First run a small sharp knife around the edge of the mold to loosen the Jell-O. Fill your sink with very hot water and briefly dip the bottom of the mold in it. Place the platter on top of the mold. Rest the mold on the towel for a second to get rid of the water, and then flip both the mold and the platter over so that the platter is now on the bottom. You might have to bang the mold a few times to encourage it to give up the Jell-O. If this fails, rinse the towel with very hot water, wring it out, and spread it over the mold for a moment. See, I told you it was easier to serve it from a glass bowl.

Garnish with purple grapes and fresh mint leaves, if available, or slices of apricots.

Serves 16

Ginger Biscuits

¾ cup solid vegetable
  shortening
1 cup brown sugar,
  firmly packed
1 egg
¼ cup molasses
⅓ cup finely chopped
  candied ginger

2½ cups flour, measured after
  sifting
2 teaspoons baking soda
1 teaspoon cinnamon
1 teaspoon powdered ginger
½ teaspoon powdered cloves
½ teaspoon salt
Granulated sugar

Cream the shortening and add the sugar. Mix until smooth. Beat in the egg, molasses, and ginger. Sift the flour together with the baking soda, spices, and salt. Mix into the egg mixture, combining thoroughly. Divide the dough into two portions, cover with plastic wrap, and chill for 30 minutes.

Preheat the oven to 375 degrees with the rack in the center position. Butter (or use vegetable shortening) to coat two baking sheets. Form balls of dough the size of walnuts, press the top into the granulated sugar. Place the balls of dough 1½ inches apart on prepared baking sheets and then wet your hand and shake the water off onto the cookies. Repeat once. Bake for 10–12 minutes or until the biscuits are firm.

Makes 2½–3 dozen cookies

Mandlbroyt

These toasted, sliced biscuit-type cookies are made for dunking. You can make them with either hazelnuts or almonds or a mixture of both.

4 extra large eggs
1 cup granulated sugar
1 cup vegetable oil
4 cups all-purpose flour, sifted before measuring
1 teaspoon salt
4 teaspoons baking soda
2 teaspoons almond extract

1 generous cup whole hazelnuts, toasted and skinned; or 1 generous cup toasted whole almonds; or ½ cup of each mixed (see note below about toasting nuts)
⅔ cup granulated sugar mixed with 3 tablespoons cinnamon
1 egg lightly beaten with 1 tablespoon water

Preheat the oven to 350 degrees with the rack in the center position. Line 2 heavy-duty baking sheets with foil. Combine the eggs and sugar in the bowl of an electric mixer and beat for 5 minutes at high speed. Beat in the oil. Sift the dry ingredients together, and on low speed add them to the egg mixture. Add the extract and the nuts.

Knead the dough by hand on a lightly floured board, adding a bit more flour if the dough is too sticky to handle. Divide the dough into 5 portions and knead a tablespoon or so of the cinnamon sugar into each portion. Form each portion of dough into a log about 12 inches long and 2 inches wide. Place the logs on the baking sheets about 3 inches apart. Brush each log with the egg/water mixture and then sprinkle generously with the remaining cinnamon sugar.

Bake for 30 minutes. Halfway through the baking, reverse the baking sheets shelf to shelf and back to front. Cut the cookies while they are still warm, into diagonal slices about 1½ inches wide. Place the slices on their sides and return to the oven to toast for 5 minutes.

Makes 4 dozen cookies

TO TOAST NUTS

Preheat the oven to 400 degrees with the rack in the upper position. Place the nuts on a heavy-duty baking sheet and bake for 7–10 minutes, then shake the pan well to redistribute the nuts and bake another 5–10 minutes, keeping a close eye on the nuts because they will burn easily. To remove the skins from the hazelnuts, rub them with a towel while they are still hot. It is not necessary to remove every bit of skin from the hazelnuts. If you are not using the nuts right away, store them in the freezer.

Coconut Macaroons

This recipe is best made by hand and not in an electric mixer.

Vegetable oil
6 ounces almond paste
½ cup granulated sugar
½ cup confectioners sugar, sifted

1 teaspoon almond extract
2 cups sweetened shredded coconut
2 egg whites

Preheat the oven to 350 degrees with the rack in the center position. Line a baking sheet with foil and lightly coat the foil with vegetable oil. Mash together the almond paste and the two sugars and then mix in the extract and coconut. Beat the egg whites until they are foamy and then blend them into the coconut mixture, making sure all the ingredients are well combined. The dough will be sticky. Rinse your hands and then form teaspoon-sized mounds, placing them 1 inch apart on the foil. Keep your hands moist when rolling the macaroons.

Bake for 16–18 minutes or until the edges are light brown and the cookies are a golden color. If the bottoms get too brown, slip another cookie sheet under the first one.

Makes about 2 dozen macaroons

Hello

I never had to think much about the ancient Jewish ritual of circumcision until I had a baby boy of my own. First of all, growing up in a family where there were no spoken names for body parts other than those shared by both genders—arms, legs, necks, etc.—it was difficult to have a conversation between peers, never mind between generations, about one's privates; in the second place, by virtue of my age and sex, I wasn't in the need-to-know category anyway. Parental reports of assorted boy cousins' ''brisses'' (to which I was never invited) highlighted the deliciousness of the honey cake, the fine quality and/or abundance of the schnapps, or the steadiness of the mohel's hands (I thought he was the one cutting the honey cake), while studiously omitting any mention of the main event. Over the years I couldn't help but catch on, but as I said I never gave it much thought until the day after my son was born.

My mother (upon hearing the cry, ''It's a Boy!'') went into high gear. ''You need to find a mohel, a good one with a good reputation and good hands. Dad will take care of the schnapps, and I'll take care of the guest list and make the honey cake. Don't worry about what to wear—the mother isn't invited anyway.''

Completely immobilized by pain and exhaustion from birth in the cesarean manner (I had suggested naming the kid Sid to remind myself never to do this again), I lay in my hospital bed and listened to my mother with the same passive incredulousness as if she had been giving me directions for mounting a wintertime assault on the north face of Mount Everest. My eyes took on a glazed faraway look as I thought back to the less complicated days of my life—when I only had to worry about dropping my toast jelly side up. Later, during visiting hours when my husband showed up, he had the same glazed look.

"I see my mother talked to you about the bris," I said. He rolled his eyes toward the ceiling in silent reply.

At least we didn't have to worry about finding a place to have the bris. Since I had to be in the hospital ten days, we could rent Mount Sinai Hospital's special "ritual circumcision" room and the "ceremony" could take place just before my discharge. To our relief, along with the room came a short list of mohels.

"Rabbi Hyman Gross—now there's a name for a mohel," exclaimed the new father focusing in on the list. That was how we picked him—we hoped the reputation and steady hands were as good as the name. We put in a call to his office and requested his presence a week hence.

Two or three days later I was awakened from a Demerol induced sleep by a large flapping crow that had landed in a dusty heap by my bedside. Groggily I watched as the black wings flapped feebly and the feathers organized themselves into a short, slight, bent-backed elderly gentleman with a long, narrow face crowned with bushy Groucho Marx-style eyebrows. Eyebrows aside, his most startling feature was his beak, I mean nose, which crested magnificently below a pair of very thick gold-rimmed glasses—the kind people with perfect vision uncharitably refer to as Coke-bottle bottoms.

He peered at me for a moment, squinting myopically at my name on the hospital chart, checking it against the one written in his little notebook clutched in his thickly gnarled, age-spotted hand and then said, "Mudda," imperiously and in a thick Yiddish accent, pushing his glasses back up his beak with a stubby finger (where they paused only a moment before sliding right back down), "I am Rabbi Gross. Now, da rules of der game. . . ."

Bad dream, I am thinking. Drug-induced nightmare. I groped around for the nurse's call button. As if he read my mind and felt the need to instill some reality into my foggy brain, he shrugged off his long black coat and threw it over the end of the bed, trapping my feet in place. A small dust cloud rose and settled around it.

"Da rules," he continued, "are dese: Eleven o'clock prompt I start. Tell all them that vas late for da vedding, they should be early for da bris, since after twelve I charge adult rates." He sniggered at his own joke, which I found remarkable—he probably heard himself say it hundreds, thousands(?) of times and still thought it funny. Hearing it the first time I wanted to burst into tears.

Completely misconstruing my expression he assured me that I wouldn't have to witness the ordeal, since the mother isn't invited to the bris for some mystical reasons that the mother isn't privy to either.

"I need," he went on, "da names in Hebrew of der baby, da fadda, da grandfadda, da godfadda, und da mudda." He paused, looked at me expectantly. I realized he wanted those names now. The task of trying to remember everyone's Hebrew name (when I could hardly remember their English names) left me too weak to wonder where I could possibly get another mohel at such short notice.

Mercifully at this moment da fadda himself appeared in the doorway. Seeing that he might have a live one on hand, the rabbi turned his full attention to David and started reading him "da rules of der game." I closed my eyes in relief, waiting for my husband to tell this character that we preferred to wait for the rabbi from central casting . . .the one with the fancy three-piece suit, gold watch chain slung across his vest, perfect eyesight, manicured nails, rock-steady hands, and a Lincoln Continental parked out front. I dozed off secure in the knowledge that my husband was telling the half-blind, spastic Rabbi Hyman Foreskin (I had renamed him more appropriately, I felt) that he simply wasn't what we had in mind. When I awoke David was standing in the door shaking hands with the rabbi.

"Well, that's taken care of," he said, walking back to my bedside.

"You told him we were getting someone else," I said.

"Hell, no. Why would we want someone else? This guy's the genuine article. He's done thousands of brisses—he even circumcised one of the Roosevelt babies."

"Teddy or Franklin?" I shrieked. "How could you consider letting someone old enough to operate on someone born that long ago touch our baby? This guy can hardly walk and talk at the same time. Genuine article is right—he's probably the world's oldest surviving mohel. There's no way I'll let him near my son with a knife in his hand."

David rang the nurse for more painkiller (did he think codeine would quell angst?) and then patiently explained to me that it was the consensus of my obstetrician, the head nurse, and the two mothers in the next room (who had used Rabbi Gross for their first sons' circumcisions) that the guy was tops in his field. "Besides," he hastened to assure me, "he doesn't use a knife, there's this little gizmo. . . ." His hands moved around like he was using a small can opener, but then he stopped when I indicated that I didn't want to hear anymore by turning a very serious shade of green.

Since I felt that I had lost the major battle of this war, I gave up on every other skirmish. Just like in the delivery when it got to the point when I didn't care what anyone else did to me, I relinquished all interest and responsibility in the bris. After all, I wasn't even invited.

My mother was in her glory. From the seriousness with which she took the baking of the honey cakes, one could easily imagine her in among the hollyhocks and honeysuckle, shaking a warning forefinger at the bees, lest their honey not be up to her standards. Was it the momentous event of the arrival of the first grandchild that tipped my father momentarily off his rocker and led him to the liquor store to buy a case of schnapps to serve to nine people? As Rabbi Gross (as we later found out) was so fond of saying, "God only knows what he was thinking."

The day arrived and it was a busy one. David had borrowed his parents' car in order to chauffeur the young prince home. He reported finding a great parking space right outside the hospital. The relatives arrived from out of town and filled up my room with chatter. My mother swept in with the honey cake carefully packed in three large Lord & Taylor boxes. Where were the monogrammed napkins? My mother-in-law presented me with her box of honey cake and an outfit to take the baby home in: a long, old-fashioned starched gown with delicate lace encircling the neck and arms that my husband had worn home from the hospital. My back ached from the thought of how long it took her to hand wash and iron it and my head ached at the thought of how our baby would scream at being tortured into it. My sisters-in-law, their beautiful silk dresses rustling, oohed and aahed over the tiny undershirts from Best's, while their (real) French perfume blended with the smell of baby powder, the milk from my leaking breasts, and antiseptic cleaner jolting me temporarily back into a world I had forgotten, a world where women had time and energy to shave their legs, talk on the phone, and make a dinner that was more than one course.

I pulled my rumpled hospital gown closed a little tighter across my swollen bosom and experienced that nightmare feeling that I had come to a formal party dressed for bed. The grandfathers, out of their element in the maternity ward, hung around the door to my room waiting for the arrival of the mohel, reliving every bris they had ever attended. The arrival of the godparents and two distant cousins elevated the noise level while depleting both the oxygen level and my tolerance for this whole affair. I began to understand how some postpartum mothers couldn't be held responsible for their actions.

At this very moment, in flapped Rabbi Foreskin, saving me from humiliating myself with a flood of tears that would, without any doubt, be interpreted by the masses as my disappointment at not being included in this barbaric ritual. Truth be told, I was immensely relieved that I didn't have to be present at what I was sure would be the maiming of my firstborn. The rabbi took attendance (was I the only one who noticed how badly his hands were shaking?) and then ushered the throngs out of the room and down the hall for the ceremony. David scooped up the baby and patted me on the head. "We'll be back in ten minutes with some honey cake for you and then we can take you both home," he assured me. Liar, I thought.

I luxuriated in the silence for a moment before I took on the persona of the mother of the condemned man. Fearing the worst, wringing my hands, the first ten minutes only took an hour to pass. During the next ten minutes I was distracted by my obstetrician's discharge visit. He checked me out, assured me everything was in working order, and cautioned me that the only two things on the forbidden list were sex and stairs—for three weeks. Sex I could live without, and stairs weren't a problem since our fifth-floor apartment was reached via elevator. He left and I continued wringing my hands for what seemed like a very long time. It seemed like a very long time because, in fact, it was a goddamned long time. At the hour mark I was frantic and completely prepared for the worst when in came a nurse bearing my screaming son.

"Everything's fine. . .sort of," she said.

I reached for his diaper and she said, "No, no the baby's perfect. The mohel did a super job."

"Then what's the problem? What took so long?" I asked her.

"Here comes your husband now. It's probably better if he explains."

He with the explanation looked mighty sheepish. I noticed that he had brought neither honey cake nor the contingent of relatives with him. The baby was happily sucking away so I figured whatever had happened really didn't involve him. David assured me immediately that the mohel did indeed have rock-steady hands when it came to doing business and our son would never be embarrassed in the locker room. He paused a long time. I could see he was struggling with just how to frame the next piece of news.

"Ummmm. . .my sister Anne. The baby's aunt. . . ."

"Yes, I know your sister Anne, the baby's aunt," I said rather impatiently. What on earth was he trying to tell me?

I won't even try to retell it in his words—you people don't have enough time. Here's what happened: it seems there were two areas in the bris room—one glass-enclosed cubicle where the mohel, father, the grandfathers, and the godfather stood around a small table that held the baby and another larger area for the "audience." My sister-in-law, whom you all know by this time is named Anne, sat in the very back of the outer area—where the view was limited to the heads of the people sitting in front of you. Anne, who apparently looked out the window during the proceedings, waited for everything to be over and then passed out, hitting her head on a radiator. She was knocked out cold and had to be rushed to the hospital's emergency room. As you can imagine, my mother-in-law was extremely upset. She did not take comfort in Rabbi Hyman Foreskin's shrugging his shoulders and telling her, "It could have been something she had for breakfast, or it could have been something else. God only knows what was on her mind."

With all the ensuing hysteria, David decided that a good course of action was to get his parents' car from his great parking space and take it around to the emergency room so his sister, when she revived, wouldn't have far to walk. To his astonishment, instead of finding the car he found the hydrant that had prompted the towing of said car. A panicked call to the police produced the welcome news that seventy-five dollars in cash would result in the release of the car. Do you have any idea how much seventy-five dollars was back in 1969? It was enough for a four-course dinner for two at Lutèce's (actually that's hearsay—I myself had never eaten at Lutèce's, and after we paid this towing bill I probably never would).

So, the baby's in one piece, the sister-in-law's got a major goose egg, the mother-in-law's furious with the mohel's insensitivity, the car's being held for ransom in some godforsaken lot in the Bronx, my mother's honey cake sits untouched in the Lord & Taylor boxes. That case of schnapps was looking mighty appealing. God only knew what else could happen.

We bundled the baby (dressed sensibly in an easy-on stretch suit, the fancy ironed dress repacked for another grandchild), my mother (who was going to help out for a few days), the honey cake, and the mudda and fadda into a cab and headed off to our apartment in Brooklyn Heights, leaving behind the rest of the family to deal with concussions and confiscated cars. The baby slept peacefully in my arms, and as he made his first crossing of the Brooklyn Bridge I began to relax, thinking about how good it would feel to be home, where the crises would be confined to running out of clean diapers and dealing with a little colic. I was ready to be a mother.

Not so fast, just one more little thing. We trooped into the lobby of our building, laden with the baby, my suitcase, vases of flowers, baby paraphernalia from the hospital, and headed toward the elevator. On the door was a sign informing us that the elevator was out of order and would be for several days. My utter exhaustion combined with the obstetrician's restrictions ringing in my ears; tackling those five flights made a trek across the Sahara seem like a stroll in the park. The baby woke up and started to scream. I handed him to my mother and headed back toward the street.

"Where are you going?" my mother and husband called in alarm.

"Back to the hospital," I called over my shoulder.

"Wait," yelled my husband, "you forgot the baby!"

"Wait," yelled my mother, "take some honey cake!"

Honey Cake I

3½ cups flour, measured after sifting
1 teaspoon baking soda
3 teaspoons baking powder
1 teaspoon cinnamon
½ teaspoon nutmeg
¼ teaspoon ginger
½ teaspoon cloves
1 cup buckwheat honey
1 cup strong black coffee (instant or decaf is fine)
3 tablespoons cognac
1 teaspoon vanilla
4 extra large eggs
½ cup vegetable oil
1 cup dark brown sugar, firmly packed
2 apples, peeled, cored, and finely chopped
½ cup golden raisins
½ cup sliced almonds

Preheat the oven to 350 degrees (325 degrees if you use a glass baking dish), with the rack in the center position. Grease either 2 9 × 5-inch loaf pans or 1 large (12 × 15-inch) baking dish. Sift the flour, baking soda, baking powder, and spices together into a bowl and set aside.

In a 2-quart saucepan combine the honey and coffee and bring to a boil. Cool slightly and add the cognac and vanilla. In the bowl of an electric mixer combine the eggs, oil, sugar, and chopped apple. Mix well and add the flour mixture in 3 additions alternating with the coffee/honey mixture. Mix in the raisins. Pour into the prepared pans and sprinkle with the sliced almonds.

Bake for 1 hour, or until a toothpick inserted in the center comes out clean and dry.

Makes 2 loaves or 1 large cake to serve 12–15

Honey Cake II

1 cup dried apples, coarsely
  chopped
¼ cup brandy or applejack
Juice and grated rind of
  1 large orange
3 extra large eggs
1 cup granulated sugar
¾ cup vegetable oil
¾ cup honey

½ cup strong coffee
3 cups flour, measured after
  sifting
1 teaspoon baking soda
2 teaspoons baking powder
1 teaspoon cinnamon
1 cup raisins
1 cup walnuts, coarsely chopped
Confectioners sugar

Preheat the oven to 350 degrees with the rack in the center position. Grease and flour a 13 × 9 × 2-inch pan. Place the dried apples, the brandy or applejack, and the orange juice and grated rind in a small saucepan and simmer until the apples have absorbed most of the liquid. Set aside to cool slightly.

In the work bowl of an electric mixer or by hand beat the eggs and sugar until thick and pale yellow. Beat in the oil and honey and then the coffee. Sift together the dry ingredients (including the cinnamon) and mix them into the batter, mixing only until blended. Add the apple mixture, raisins, and walnuts.

Bake for 1 hour until the center is firm and a tester comes out dry. Cool on a rack and then either invert onto a plate or cut into squares in the pan. Dust with sifted confectioners sugar.

Makes one 9 × 13-inch cake

Shooting Stars

In the Mixmaster of my distant memory the following ingredients churn around and around: Mark Twain, shooting stars, my Aunt Sarah, and a fluffy pink birthday cake garnished with maraschino cherries. Although the rainbow Kodachrome of the images has turned to sepia over the years, I know for certain that it is more than the fact that our youngest child, Samuel, is named for my Aunt Sarah that connects them; it's the shooting stars.

That February day many years ago our first grade class had a field trip to Mark Twain's house, which is located in Hartford where I grew up. The other children were dazzled by the Tiffany glass and bronze moldings, by the ancient telephone and ornate decor. My imagination was captured by a fact told to the class by the tour guide: Mark Twain was born in a year that Halley's comet came close to the earth and died, seventy-five years later, in the year of its next appearance. That evening when I shared this fascinating piece of information with my family, my Aunt Sarah told me that she too had seen Halley's comet—in 1910 when she was seven years old—the same age I was then. She told me I would have to wait until 1985 to see the comet, but I might be able to spot a shooting star.

I remember bundling up that freezing cold February night—Sarah in her fur coat and I in my wool overcoat—and going out onto the back porch of my aunt's double-decker on Magnolia Street. Down below was an urban landscape—cars and trees and garbage cans silently entombed in ice and snow. Up above the moonless night sky was an endless black backdrop upon which God, the jeweler (Sarah's interpretation), displayed His twinkling diamonds. We leaned against the porch railing, our elbows cracking a ridge of frozen snow, and peered up, unblinking, until our eyes got dry and our toes began to grow numb. We agreed to try it again in the summer and raced inside to the warm kitchen where my cousin Leah (only four years older than I and already an accomplished cook) had just finished frosting a layer cake in honor of both her mother's, Esther, and George Washington's birthdays. This splendid concoction made with an abundance of confectioners sugar and cocktail cherries purloined from the liquor cabinet was, to a sweet lover, heaven-sent. To this day Leah's cake remains *the* birthday cake of choice in our family.

Thirty-three years later I found myself sitting on the bank of the Vermont side of Lake Champlain waiting for sunset so I could give Sam (turning four that day) his birthday present. "This year," I had promised him, "you're going to have a present you can't hold or touch, but it will be so special that you won't mind." Our acquisitive child was naturally dubious.

We sat on the cool, flat pebbles, nibbling at slices of cheddar cheese and whole-grained bread spread with a thick layer of Vermont butter. Our older boys skipped stones across the lake, which was dappled golden with the setting sun's low-slung rays. As the thin, fiery orange disk sank lower and lower in the sky, Sam, the ever-tireless inquisitor, took up his interrogation.

"Mommy, why can't I keep the present?"

"It's too big."

"But can I try to carry it?"

"No, you can't even reach it."

"But I can bring the big ladder from the cellar."

"Nope, that's not high enough."

"I can sit on Daddy's shoulders."

"Still not high enough. Stop asking—you'll have to wait and when you see it, you'll understand."

By this time the sun was gone. The older boys had started a bonfire. The August night was still and hot and the water, gently lapping the shore, looked cool and inviting. The boys took the canoe out and dove off the ends, making the loudest whoops and the biggest splashes they could, while the adults waded out slowly, immersing themselves in the cool and inky darkness of the lake. Floating on my back I watched the flames of the bonfire weave and dance against the pines that lined the shore. As the flames caught the bone-dry kindling, I could see tiny, brilliant sparks shoot skyward, going up to help make Sam's special present.

There was a rush for towels as the shivering swimmers stepped out of the velvety water and into the night air. I trekked up to the house to get Leah's cake, wishing that Sarah could share this moment. Then wrapped and snug by the fire we sang "Happy Birthday" to Sam, who screwed up his face to make a giant wish and then did a mighty job of blowing out the candles. He looked at his parents expectantly and we said, "Just a few more moments until your present." He did a masterful job of cutting, serving (the birthday person's honor), and devouring several slices of cake.

For a while the only noise to be heard was the high-speed whine of cicadas and an occasional mournful loon. The fire lit up the faces of my family intently licking the last bits of pink frosting from their forks and the corners of their mouths.

"The night is as dark as chocolate," noted one boy.

"I'll eat the Milky Way next," added another.

David and I dispatched the kids to find marshmallow toasting sticks. Upon their return we, quite patronizingly, supervised them in the art of perfect toasting; an even, medium-brown on the outside and completely melted on the inside. We were forced to eat dozens of mistakes and "almosts" before they got the hang of it.

"Sam," we told him, "to see your present we have to move far away from the campfire, to where it's really dark."

There was a debate about the best place to sit—farther down the beach versus the canoe in the middle of the lake. Sam, nervous about the tippiness of the canoe, opted for the beach, so we packed up our towels and set off. As soon as we rounded a bend and the fire was out of sight, we spread out our towels and lay down on the smooth pebbles.

"OK, Sam," I said, "your present is going to appear up in the sky. You have to watch carefully to see it."

"What are we looking for?" he wanted to know. "I can't even see the moon."

"That's good," I said. "The moon would make it harder to see."

"How will I know what to look for?"

"Believe me, you'll know. Come on and lie down so you can see the sky."

Sam snuggled between us like a tiny sardine in a hero roll. His father pointed out the constellations of the summer sky:

triangular Lyra, the Herdsman, the Scorpion, and the Big and Little Dippers. We showed him the silver, fairy-dusted Milky Way and Venus hovering on the horizon. Jets from Burlington bound for New York (or Paris) blinked their red lights at us. Sam waved and wanted to know if the pilot had waved back.

We pointed out a tiny satellite moving purposefully in its orbit above us.

"Where's the present?" Sam was growing restive. I hoped that I hadn't made a big mistake.

"Keep watching, you'll see," we assured him.

Two bullfrogs seemed to be courting within arm's reach, their croaking vibrating in our ears.

"Ribbit!" said Sam, trying to bug out his eyes like a frog.

"Knee-deep," I replied in my faux baritone.

We took turns doing our bullfrog imitations without taking our eyes off the heavens. It was hard to keep up the level of intensity, the muscles holding my eyes so wide open began to tire, and I found my mind drifting back to a night four years ago, a few days after Sam was born. Neither of us had been able to sleep because of the sticky heat. I had paced back and forth, up and down the hall outside our bedroom, cradling him close to my breasts swollen with milk that he didn't seem interested in drinking. We went downstairs to the rocking chair to give that a try, but something led me past the parlor and out onto the porch. The night was inky black with no moon. There was no breeze to rustle the limp maple leaves. Some Fourth of July revelers had taken a rock to the streetlight in front of our house and the city had not yet gotten around to fixing it, so I was able to see the night sky quite clearly. Suddenly across the sky flashed a shooting star. Its brilliance and duration astonished me. It hung in its path for a moment before disappearing into the Milky Way. Another followed and then another. For over an hour I watched with wonder as the stars streaked around the sky as if flung by an invisible slingshot. It was the Perseid, August's annual meteor shower.

"Look, baby," I whispered to Sam, who had finally fallen into a peaceful sleep, "the stars are flying just for you. Someday when you're a big boy, you can watch them with me." It seemed Sarah's way of sending a greeting from heaven to her tiny namesake.

Now I turned my head to look at my big boy snuggled close to me on the shore of Lake Champlain. He was absentmindedly scratching a mosquito bite on one of his bony knees. His eyes were glazed with the sleep that comes from hours of hard playing in the water, and his eyelids were at half-mast. A sudden movement registered in the corner of my eye and made me yell and jerk my finger skyward. His eyes flew open and he caught the next one zinging out of the Milky Way toward the horizon.

The Perseid was in full and silent show. Every fifteen seconds or so one shot across the star-dusted sky looking for all the world like a delicate strip of phosphorescent white neon. Awed by the spectacle, mouth gaping in wonder, gasping with each burst across the sky, Sam's eyes, now bugging out more than the bullfrog's, took it all in.

After a few moments his moist hand crept into mine and he whispered in my ear, "Mommy, will the stars fall on us?"

"No, baby, they won't ever fall on us. They are taking your birthday wishes up to heaven."

Sam screwed up his freckled face, shut his eyes tight in preparation to make his wishes.

"Are you sure I shouldn't wish that they won't fall on us?"

"They won't fall on us."

Thus reassured, his body relaxed and he made his wishes.

Later, as his dad carried him up to the house, the sleepy birthday boy with the marshmallow mustache said that he had loved his present and wanted the very same thing again next year. I told him that I was sure it could be arranged.

Leah's Cherry Cake

This simple recipe is a good one to use to teach yourself or someone else how to bake a cake. I've made it with my children—perhaps you know a child who would enjoy learning how to bake a cake from scratch. The cake is on the sweet side and thoroughly and refreshingly unsophisticated.

FOR THE CAKE LAYERS

2 cups plus 1 tablespoon flour, measured after sifting
3 teaspoons baking powder
½ teaspoon salt
½ cup solid vegetable shortening (such as Crisco)
1¼ cups granulated sugar
20 maraschino cherries (approximately), cut in eighths (about ⅔ cups)
¼ cup maraschino cherry juice
½ cup milk
4 extra large egg whites

Preheat the oven to 350 degrees with the rack in the center position. Grease 2 8-inch or 9-inch cake pans, line them with rounds of parchment or waxed paper, grease the paper, and then thoroughly dust the pans with flour, knocking out the excess. Sift together the flour, baking powder, and salt and set aside.

In the bowl of an electric mixer cream the shortening and the sugar. Mix in the cherries, cherry juice, and milk. The batter will look curdled—that's OK. Add the dry ingredients and mix well.

Add the egg whites and beat on moderate speed for 2 minutes. Spread the batter into the prepared pans and bake for 25–30 minutes or until the tops are golden brown and the sides start pulling away from the pan.

Turn the layers out onto cake racks, peel off the parchment or wax paper, and cool completely before frosting with the following icing.

FLUFFY CHERRY ICING

4 ounces cream cheese at
  room temperature
¼ cup butter at room
  temperature
2½–3 cups confectioners
  sugar, sifted

2–3 tablespoons heavy cream
1–2 tablespoons maraschino
  cherry juice (approximately)
8 maraschino cherries,
  cut in half

In the bowl of an electric mixer combine the cream cheese and butter and beat until light and fluffy. Add the confectioners sugar and beat until well blended. Add enough heavy cream to get the frosting to a spreading consistency and then dribble in enough cherry juice to tint the frosting a light pink. Take care not to overbeat it at this point since it may separate.

Spread a small amount of the icing on top and smooth it over the layer. Cover with the second layer. Spread the rest of the frosting over the top and sides of the cake. Garnish with the cherries.

Makes 1 2-layer 8-inch or 9-inch cake

The Ladies' Nostalgia Dinner

Funny how some foods simply go out of style. Corned beef, move over for carpaccio, radishes, make way for radicchio. Surely some foods deserved to disappear—one look at any cover of any *Gourmet* magazine from the sixties and a whole list of dishes that never should have seen the light of day come flooding to mind: unnaturally rose-colored boiled shrimp nestled on a bed of dead white rice, napped with an unearthly pastel green flour-based sauce. How about a brilliantly polished ornate silver chafing dish brimming with gray Swedish meatballs swimming in a sweet-and-sour sauce that boasts grape jelly as one of its main ingredients? Yes, happily *Gourmet* deposited those foods in the garbage disposals of the sixties and went on to bigger and tastier things—but what on earth happened to Nesselrode pie? Did it somehow get dumped along with the meatballs and the yucky green sauce?

Someone made a big mistake and I would really like to know who. Who was it that decided that my favorite nonchocolate dessert wasn't chic enough to make it into the eighties where my children could learn to love it too? Was it the same creep who got a bug in his ear about Waldorf salad, cream cheese sandwiches on date nut bread, and mimosa (no, not the drink—the salad made with red Jell-O, bits of orange sections, and miniature marshmallows)?

When I was a little girl, Scoler's Restaurant on Farmington Avenue in West Hartford, Connecticut, made the quintessential Nesselrode pie. It was about a mile-high slice of pure heaven; thick rum-flavored custard lightened with whipped cream and studded with candied red and green cherries and angelica. Now, truth to tell, I hated the green cherries and angelica and used to make a neat pile of those pieces on the side of my plate, but the rest of it was absolutely perfect. It used to wobble slightly when the waitress set it down in front of me, and I in turn would almost quiver in anticipation of the smooth, sweet rum-flavored filling melting across my tongue. My fork would sink halfway down its stem into the filling, and the thin flaky crust would melt in my mouth. Even after eating a whole plate of fried salami and eggs or a hot turkey sandwich with mashed potatoes and gravy, I could still put away an entire piece of that pie and have room left over to finish that of any family member who was flagging when I had cleaned my plate.

Don't you ever long for the good old days when French fries weren't all exactly the same shape and size and didn't come directly from a freezer bag to the fryolator? Well, once every year my longings are fulfilled at my house at the annual Ladies' Nostalgia Dinner, to which my women friends are invited to come for supper and bring an adored dish from their childhoods. Tremendous energy goes into researching authentic recipes, revivals, and/or creative adaptations of things that were remembered as wonderful in childhood, but leave an adult palate wondering what the fuss was all about. For weeks before the event the phone lines between Boston and home are burning. Calls go out to Grand Rapids for Mom's pea soup, to Biloxi for Granny's chicken and dumplings, to Bar Harbor for Dad's way of fixing his special fish chowder, to Sioux City for Aunt Sue's anise melt-away cookies, and to Cousin Ethel in Fort Myers, who makes the world's best key lime pie.

All the courses are set on the table at once, buffet style, and the first event is to "Name that Dish!" The air is filled with cries of, "Oh, my God! Chipped beef on toast—that's the last meal I ever served my first husband." "Is that Spanish rice?" "Apricot Jell-O mold—we had that at my wedding." My sophisticated friends who know and can pronounce the names of every triple-creme cheese manufactured in France and pick wines to match them pile their plates high with tuna noodle casserole, Jell-O mold, Swiss steak, and noodles with sour cream and cottage cheese. Mouths that clamp down at the thought of the number of calories in a piece of plain grilled scrod open wide in delight at another serving of sweet-and-sour stuffed cabbage and cheese blintzes topped with blueberry sauce and sour cream.

We enjoy these lovely and love-filled foods that zing us backwards in time to a place where Mom was always in the kitchen, an apron tied around her waist, filling the cookie jar with homemade goodies and smiling while she served up steaming hot made-from-scratch meals three times a day. Did we all grow up in Springfield, USA, along with the Andersons of "Father Knows Best"? Sure we did, in our memories, at least, and as we dig into a piece of banana cream pie or wipe a crumb of three-layer chocolate sour cream cake from the corners of our mouths. We are even able to convince ourselves that Mom didn't even own a can opener, never mind a recipe for the infamous canned fried onion ring, green bean, and cream of mushroom soup casserole. For one evening we are all able to convince ourselves that this stuff isn't fattening, oversalted, and generally not in the best interest of our digestive systems.

Every year after the Ladies' Nostalgia Dinner I promise myself that I'll make the kids a Nesselrode pie. Every year I look at the long recipe, the amount of fat and sugar in it, and every year I tuck the recipe away in the back of the file box. I am shocked and dismayed, but I have to come face-to-face with the bitter truth—I'm the one who did in Nesselrode pie. I think I'll begin to try to repair the damage I've done. Kids—Nesselrode pie for dessert tonight!

Stuffed Cabbage

2–3 quarts water
1 head of cabbage—about
3 pounds

TO PREPARE THE CABBAGE

Fill a large pot with water and bring to a boil. Use a sharp
knife to cut deeply around the core of the cabbage to help loosen
and detach the leaves while cooking. Place the cabbage in the
boiling water, cover the pot, and simmer for 20–30 minutes or
until the leaves are tender and appear to be loosening from the
head. Meanwhile, prepare the sauce.

FOR THE SAUCE

¼ cup vegetable oil
2 large onions, coarsely
chopped
2 large cloves garlic, minced
1 28-ounce can whole tomatoes
in puree or the equivalent
amount of crushed tomatoes

1 15-ounce can tomato sauce
3 tablespoons brown sugar
3 tablespoons granulated
sugar
1 tablespoon lemon juice
Salt and pepper to taste

In a Dutch oven heat the oil and sauté the onion until lightly
browned, then add the garlic and cook for another minute, taking care not to burn the garlic. Add the tomatoes and the sauce.
If you use whole tomatoes mash them with a fork or puree in
a food processor or blender. Stir in the two sugars and the lemon
juice. Season to taste with salt and pepper.

FOR THE MEAT FILLING

2 slices white bread
1 large onion, finely chopped
¼ cup vegetable oil
1½ cups ground beef

1 egg
½ teaspoon salt
Freshly ground pepper to taste

Soak the bread briefly in water, squeeze out the water, and
crumble the bread. Sauté the onion in oil until it is lightly
browned. Add the beef and cook over moderate heat until it is

well browned. Break it up into small pieces with a wooden spoon.
Off the heat mix in the egg, the bread, and salt and pepper.

TO ASSEMBLE

½ cup raisins

When the cabbage is cooked, remove from the pot and drain
well. Rinse under cold water before trying to peel off the individual leaves. Carefully peel off the cabbage leaves and line them
up on your work space. For each leaf use approximately 1 heaping tablespoon of meat filling. Roll the filling into a ball and place
it at the narrow end of the cabbage leaf. Roll it once, folding
in the sides, and then continue rolling to make a neat package.

Place 1 layer of rolls seam side down in a heavy casserole. Ladle
on some sauce and scatter on some raisins. When you get down
to the smaller leaves double them up, overlapping to make small
rolls. Place another layer on top and repeat with the sauce and
raisins until you have layered all the rolls.

Ladle the remaining sauce on top. Top with the remaining
raisins. Cover the casserole and simmer on low/moderate heat
for 40 minutes.

This dish is best prepared in advance and then reheated when
ready to serve. Serve over rice.

Serves 6

Banana Cream Pie

FOR THE CRUST

1 tablespoon butter or Crisco—
  for greasing the pie plate
1½ cups graham cracker crumbs

⅓ cup (⅔ stick) sweet (unsalted)
  butter, melted
3 tablespoons granulated sugar
¼ teaspoon salt

Use the butter or Crisco to grease the pie plate. Preheat the oven to 375 degrees with the rack in the center position. Combine all the ingredients and mix well. Use your fingers to press the crumbs into the prepared pie plate, making sure that the rim is not too thin. Bake for 20 minutes until the crust is dried and slightly browned. Cool completely before filling.

FOR THE BANANA CUSTARD FILLING

1 cup milk
4 large egg yolks
1 cup granulated sugar
4 tablespoons flour
1 tablespoon cornstarch

4 tablespoons sweet (unsalted)
  butter, cut in chunks
½ teaspoon cinnamon
2 ripe bananas
1½ cups heavy cream

Scald the milk in a 1½-quart heavy saucepan. Remove from heat. Beat the egg yolks and the sugar until the mixture is thick and pale yellow. Beat in the flour and cornstarch. Slowly mix in the hot milk. Transfer the mixture back to the saucepan set over medium heat and stir with a wire whip, constantly taking care to scrape the bottom and sides of the pan to keep the custard from burning. The mixture will thicken and get lumpy. Lower the heat slightly and continue to stir vigorously for 2–3 more minutes or until the mixture begins to smooth out. Remove the pan from the heat, stir in the butter, mixing until it melts. Stir in the cinnamon.

Mash 1 of the bananas and stir it into the custard. Cool the custard completely. Slice the remaining banana and layer it on the bottom of the pie shell.

Whip the cream and fold half of it into the cooled custard. Pour the filling into the pie shell. Garnish with the remaining whipped cream.

Makes 1 9-inch pie serving 8–10

Waldorf Salad

The addition of fennel, fresh ginger, and curry powder updates this classic American dish.

½ cup mayonnaise
½ cup sour cream
1 teaspoon curry powder
1 bulb fresh fennel, greens
  and stalks trimmed off, diced
Grated rind of 1 lemon
Juice of 1 lemon
3 Granny Smith apples,
  peeled and diced

3 stalks celery, diced
2 seedless tangerines or
  Clementines, each segment
  cut in half
1 cup red grapes, halved and
  pitted
2 tablespoons fresh ginger,
  finely julienned
⅓ cup chopped parsley

Combine the mayonnaise, sour cream, and curry powder in a small bowl and mix well. Place the fennel in a large bowl and sprinkle it with the lemon rind and juice. Add all the other ingredients to the dressing. Mix well.

Serves 6–8

Key Lime Pie

I have started to find bottled key lime juice in my grocery store. If you are lucky enough to find it, substitute it for the lime juice listed below.

FOR THE CRUMB CRUST

⅔ cup graham cracker crumbs
⅔ cup chocolate wafers, crushed
(I use Famous Chocolate Wafers, available in grocery stores)
⅓ cup sugar
1 stick sweet (unsalted) butter, melted

Preheat the oven to 375 degrees with the rack in the center position. Place the cracker and cookie crumbs and sugar in a mixing bowl, add the melted butter, and work with your fingers or a fork to blend well. Press into a lightly greased 10-inch pie pan (I use a deep Pyrex pan for this recipe). Bake 15 minutes and then cool.

FOR THE FILLING

6 extra large egg yolks
14 ounces condensed milk
½ cup heavy cream
6 ounces freshly squeezed lime juice or 6 ounces Key Lime juice
1 tablespoon finely grated lime rind

Combine all the above ingredients and mix well. Pour into the prepared pie shell and bake in a 350-degree oven for about 20 minutes or until the filling is set. Cool. Add the topping below just before serving.

FOR THE TOPPING

1 cup heavy cream
2 tablespoons granulated sugar
1 teaspoon vanilla
1 tablespoon finely grated rind of 1 lime
1 thinly sliced lime

Whip the cream until it holds soft peaks. Beat in the sugar, vanilla, and lime rind. Spread over the cooled pie or pipe with a pastry bag fitted with a star tip. Decorate with slices of lime.

Serves 10–12

Three-Layer Chocolate Sour Cream Cake
with Fudge Frosting

½ cup boiling water
4 ounces unsweetened
  chocolate, chopped
1½ sticks (6 ounces) sweet
  (unsalted) butter
2 cups granulated sugar
3 extra large eggs
2 cups flour, measured after
  sifting

½ teaspoon salt
1 teaspoon baking powder
1 teaspoon baking soda
1½ cups (12 ounces)
  sour cream
1 teaspoon vanilla

Preheat the oven to 350 degrees. Set the racks to divide the oven into thirds with the racks not on the very lowest, or very highest, settings. Grease 3 8-inch cake pans, line the pans with parchment, grease the parchment, and then lightly dust the pans with flour. Pour the boiling water over the chocolate and stir until the chocolate is melted. Cream the butter and sugar together until light and fluffy. Add the eggs, one at a time, beating well after each addition. Mix in the melted chocolate.

Sift together the flour, salt, baking powder, and baking soda and mix them in 3 additions, alternating with the sour cream, into the chocolate mixture. Stir in the vanilla. Mix only until well blended. Overbeating will cause air bubbles and make the cake tough.

Pour the batter into the prepared pans and tap firmly on the counter to remove any air pockets. Bake for 40–45 minutes, rotating the positions of the pans once halfway through the baking time. The cakes are done when the sides have begun to pull away from the pans and a cake tester or toothpick inserted in the center comes out clean.

Let the layers rest in the pans for 5 minutes before turning them out onto racks. Cool completely or freeze to facilitate handling the layers before covering with the following chocolate fudge frosting.

FOR THE FUDGE FROSTING

¾ stick (3 ounces) sweet
(unsalted) butter
4 ounces unsweetened
chocolate, chopped

3 cups confectioners sugar,
(approximately), sifted
½ cup sour cream
1 teaspoon vanilla
2 tablespoons hot water

In the top of a double boiler set over gently simmering water melt the butter and chocolate together. Transfer to the bowl of an electric mixer and add the sugar, sour cream, vanilla, and hot water. Beat slowly at first and then increase the speed to high and beat until smooth and thickened. Add more sifted confectioners sugar to thicken a bit more, if necessary.

Spread a thin layer of frosting between each cake layer and then cover the sides and top with the remaining frosting.

Serves 10–12

Nesselrode Pie

I took the liberty of making optional the addition of glacé fruits, although they are traditional for this recipe. When I make this pie I substitute pieces of glacéed chestnuts, which are, unfortunately, harder to find and more expensive than the fruits. However, the good news is that the chestnuts last a long, long time and they are wonderfully delicious. I prefer a crumb crust with this pie, but you can certainly substitute a regular baked pie shell.

FOR THE CRUST

¾ cup graham cracker crumbs   ⅓ cup sugar
¾ cup finely crushed   ⅓ cup melted butter
   chocolate wafers

Preheat the oven to 350 degrees with the rack in the center position. Grease a 10-inch pie plate. Combine all the ingredients and mix well. Press into the prepared pie plate and bake for 8 minutes. Cool completely.

FOR THE FILLING

¼ cup dark rum   ¾ cup dark brown sugar,
1 envelope gelatin   firmly packed
4–5 glacéed chestnuts *or*   1 cup whole milk
   4 tablespoons glacéed fruits   ¼ cup sweetened chestnut puree
3 eggs, separated   ¼ cup granulated sugar
                                   ½ cup heavy cream

Place the rum in a small pan and sprinkle the gelatin over it. Stir until the gelatin dissolves and then place the pan over low heat and stir constantly, just until the gelatin liquefies. Do not boil. Set aside. If you use the glacéed chestnuts cut them into small pieces and set aside.

Beat the egg yolks and brown sugar together until the mixture is thick. Scald the milk and pour onto the egg mixture, combine, and then return the mixture to the pan and stir constantly over low heat until the custard just starts to thicken and coats a spoon. Immediately strain into a clean bowl, mix in the chestnut puree, and cool for 30 minutes or until the gelatin starts to set up. I pour the mixture into a shallow pan so that it cools much faster.

Whip the egg whites with the sugar until they hold soft peaks. Whip the cream. Combine the meringue and the whipped cream. Fold in the cooled custard and the glacéed chestnuts or the fruit. Pour into the prepared shell, mounding the center slightly higher than the sides. Cool at least 8 hours or overnight.

FOR THE GARNISH

½ cup heavy cream
3 tablespoons dark rum
3 tablespoons extrafine sugar

Grated bittersweet or
semisweet chocolate

Whip the cream, adding the rum and sugar when the cream holds firm peaks. Spoon or pipe, using a pastry bag fitted with medium-star tube, a border around the edge of the pie. Sprinkle with grated chocolate.

Serves 10

Springerle

Along one long wall of my kitchen are delft blue Formica shelves that the previous owner of this house designed to display her prodigious collection of sterling silver mint julep cups. It was clear that from her point of view something important should be stored here. From my point of view it needed to be something that wouldn't show the dust (I didn't own enough silver to make a display). I had the perfect thing: my collection of dozens of wooden springerle and shortbread cookie molds and butter stamps. These treasured molds had resided in an old cardboard box in our other house and were taken out and employed only once a year at Christmastime so that I could re-create a Christmas memory that existed a long time ago.

The seeds of this fantasy were planted when we first moved to Boston and I met the Slater family. They lived in a red-tiled stone castle in the country. The house had everything a transplanted New Yorker thought a castle in the country should have: sweeping lawns, groves of fruit trees, stables, grape arbors, a swimming/skating pond, rose gardens, a thicket of blackberry brambles, and best of all, the most wonderful country kitchen where my friend Karen Slater opened up to me a whole new world of culinary possibilities.

In this large, modern, but friendly room decorated in an unusual mixture of cool Scandinavian blues, greens, and purples dashed with white cabinets and stainless steel counters, Karen baked like other people read books or drive cars or do the tango—with a thoughtless and effortless grace and ease and organization that left others breathless with admiration. Strange and wonderful things were always popping in and out of her oven: rye bread made with potatoes and caraway seeds, fruit pies that rose to majestic heights and stayed there even after they were cut into, and, wonder of wonders, a pasty white spongy mass that went into her microwave oven looking like something forgotten in the back of the refrigerator and came out in the form of English muffin bread. There was monkey bread, sugar glazed Danish rings heavy with golden raisins and slivers of toasted almonds, and chewy, crusty sourdough loaves made from a starter that was rumored to be in her family for several generations. She was the first really innovative and courageous cook I had ever met (she was the first person I ever saw make homemade pasta and pizza—in 1971!), and I credit her with much of what I know and love about food today.

The best time to be at the Slaters' was Christmas, when Karen made Christmas cookies. The counters were littered with dozens of painted round and square tins waiting for their tenants to cool before being packed up inside. The table was piled high with racks of Moravian ginger cookies, Mexican wedding cakes, brandy snaps, snowballs, and chocolate rum balls. There were tray upon tray of sugar cookies that the children were in the process of decorating with colored sugar, icing, and silver balls. The heavenly smell of this Christmas kitchen combined with the perfume of freshly made popcorn waiting to be eaten or strung—whatever your pleasure—and just-brewed extra strong coffee drew you in from the wintry New England weather that gusted outside.

Boots of every size and shape, dripping melting snow, were piled haphazardly around every door. The Christmas tree presided—reigned is more accurate—in the enormous living room (large enough to accomodate the tallest and fullest Christmas tree imaginable and a concert grand piano). It was festooned with not only hundreds of glittering ornaments, but with drawings tied on with yarn and tiny painted wooden toys, candy canes and cookies. As beautiful as the tree was it was impossible to linger too long in the living room if Karen was baking in the kitchen. The genies that gently but persistently tugged me toward that big blue room in the back of the house were ginger and molasses and cardamom and caramelized sugar, bitter almond, brandy, butter, and vanilla. I would pour myself a mug of coffee, top it off with a generous amount of light cream, find a stool, and drag it over to the counter next to where Karen was mixing up the next batch of cookies. If I were really lucky she would be making springerle. These were far and away my very favorite kind. The dough, flavored with anise seeds and anise extract, was rolled out onto a floured board and then stamped with wooden molds depicting an assortment of Christmas themes: a tree, a reindeer, a candle topped with a star, an elf, Santa. Each mold left its impression on the dough, and when the cookies baked each became a tiny Christmas portrait.

Even though it's been almost seventeen years since I sat in that kitchen watching my beautiful, graceful friend roll and cut and decorate the cookies, I can recall the feel and smell and gentle rhythms of the time as if it were yesterday. The windows would be fogged and dripping with moisture from the oven's heat. The dog, a strange-looking poodle named Spooky, who looked like he had been coiffed by a blind barber and anatomically re-arranged by a speeding car, would be unobtrusively scrounging the floor for bits of dough, the wind would swirl the drifts outside up and over the lower panes of the French doors in the dining room, and the sunlight would catch and reflect bits of green and blue Danish glass that were propped against Karen's windowsill. Somewhere far away upstairs someone was rehearsing lines for a Christmas play or practicing the flute or the trumpet. Children, cheeks frost kissed and ablaze, tumbled in and out of the house and into the kitchen, their mittens encrusted with snow, their noses dripping, and their appetites roaring.

Our family felt lucky to be counted as part of the Slater household on Christmas Day. I would be hard-pressed to choose a favorite from among all the events that took place that day: tobogganing down the long front lawn at death-defying speeds blinded by the snow spray; sitting by the tree drinking brandy-spiked eggnog while listening to Karen's husband, Jonathan, read *A Child's Christmas in Wales*, followed by carols (their family knew all the words to all the verses); the Christmas feast that left us with only enough energy to sprawl on the floor and watch a Technicolor print of *Kidnapped*. At the quiet end of the day when twilight had dimmed both the world's light and the childrens' energy they crept upstairs to compare presents and try to figure out directions to multiparted toys. The exhausted grown-ups would sit in the darkened living room, propped up against one another in stockinged feet, by the fire, alternately hypnotized by the flames and then spurred to reminisce about something last week or last year or a Christmas long ago. We all agreed it had been a perfect day. At this point one of us would steal into the kitchen and return with a tin of cookies and perhaps a box of ribbon candy. And even though we had all eaten to excess, it was impossible to keep our hands from reaching for just one more gingerbread star, just one more rum ball, just one more springerle. . . .

The summer they sold that house and moved to New York it just about broke my heart. At the yard sale to get rid of twenty rooms and an attic full of stuff they couldn't cram into a Manhattan brownstone, I poked through decades of old bicycles; stacks of board games, their boxes held together with masking tape; box upon box of well-read books and records; racks of dated ball gowns; and bags of baby clothes and pieces and parts of things that made up God knew what whole when they were first bought. The boxes of things from the kitchen depressed me the most. I ran my fingers over the dusty tops of fish poachers, cake pans, Dutch ovens, and canisters. I made a small pile of things I wanted, things I felt would connect me to the memory of the happy times in this house: a white china Melitta coffeepot with a cracked top, a doll-sized copper pan for melting butter, a timer with a noise that the kids described as "someone stepping on a large frog," the corn popper—black and greasy and smelling like Christmas in the heat of August. In the last box I found the springerle molds. I was shocked and disappointed that Karen wanted to get rid of them; was there to be a new, sophisticated Christmas in New York City that didn't include cookies? I held them out to Karen and asked if she really meant to sell them.

"So that's where they are," she said. "I set them aside for you to have since they're your favorite, and I guess they got mixed up with the things to be sold. I'm glad you found them—now it's your turn to make them." Thus the torch was passed.

The second week of December I make the anise dough and take down my wooden molds (the collection has grown from the six she gave me to well over eighty). Before I get to work I call Karen (now she lives in Chicago). We laugh about making the cookies without children at our feet. We try to laugh about the fact that the next young ones in our kitchens will be grandchildren.

Now I have the country kitchen (not in a castle, I'm sorry to say), and she talks about looking forward to moving back here. We say how much we miss each other, and I promise to take good care of the cookie molds until she's ready to reclaim them. Soon, I hope.

Springerle

You need a heavy-duty electric mixer to make this dough.

6 cups all-purpose flour, measured after sifting	3 cups sugar
1½ teaspoons baking powder	Grated rind of 2 lemons
¾ teaspoon salt	3 tablespoons anise seed
4 extra large eggs	3 teaspoons anise extract

Sift the dry ingredients and set aside. In the bowl of an electric mixer beat the eggs, sugar, lemon rind, and anise seed for 15–20 minutes until the mixture is very light and fluffy. Add the extract. On low speed beat in the flour a cup at a time, taking care to incorporate each cupful before adding the next one. Divide the dough into 5–6 portions, dust each lightly with flour, and press flat between 2 sheets of plastic wrap. Try to press the dough evenly to a thickness of about ⅝ inch. This will save time rolling out the dough the next day. Wrap so that no edges are exposed to air and refrigerate for at least 12 hours.

Place the dough on a lightly floured board. If you managed to flatten it out before chilling, then don't bother rolling it further. If it is of uneven thickness, use a floured rolling pin to even it up. Flour the dough and use regular cookie cutters or wooden springerle molds to stamp out designs. Cut the cookies apart and place on a lightly greased baking sheet. Leave overnight at room temperature.

Preheat the oven to 325 degrees with the rack in the center position. Use a soft brush to brush away any excess flour left on top of the cookies. Bake the cookies 1 tray at a time for 13–15 minutes or just until they are beginning to color very slightly. Cool on racks and store in tins when completely cool.

Makes about 4 dozen, depending on the size of the molds used

Fried Chicken

With the exception of my grandmother (who cooked everything in a frying pan with lots of grease) no one did a lot of frying around our house (that goes for most of the houses I ate at during my childhood—it just wasn't the "New England way"). Even things that were in fact fried had other names—fried eggs were "over easy." Consequently, the pleasures of fried chicken were something denied me until I was grown.

Even though fried chicken is a traditionally southern dish, my first and most memorable—make that unforgettable—experience with it occured in upstate New York.

At the end of each summer for the past fifteen years, David and I and whatever children are available have made a seven-hour pilgrimage to Delaware County to a tiny town called Andes, where our friends Fern and Stuart Fisher have their country house. Whoever named Andes must have been impressed, as we are each time we see them, by the magnificent western Catskills that rise majestically above mist-filled valleys, making one think they could be in South America...if South America had green pastures filled with apple orchards, brown-and-white cows, white farmhouses, and red barns.

The Fishers discovered this heavenly peaceful retreat when they were looking for a weekend and summer place to counterbalance their hustle-bustle lives in New York City. They bought a hundred-plus-year-old parsonage on a narrow country road seven miles from town and a million miles from the day-to-day stress and ferocious pace of their day-to-day lives. The narrow white house with its screened-in porch, steeply pitched roof, and bay windows looking out over acres of pasture and mountainside sends us welcome home signals every time we pull in the drive. The house is simple—they bought it with all the original furnishings including dressers, beds, dishes, an old piano, books, and an ancient white enameled coal kitchen stove that they used to use to heat the house until the fire warden suggested that it one day might be the cause of the ultimate fire.

Over the years we used our trips to Andes to explore in depth the beautiful and diverse areas that make up New York State, and we were thrilled that our eldest son, feeling the same warm affection for the area, chose to go to college not so far away from the Fishers' country house.

Last fall we planned the annual trip to visit our friends in connection with taking Jonathan back to Vassar, which meant we would arrive in Andes a few days earlier than they. We spent the time roaming the back roads of the Catskills visiting towns with names like Phoenicia and Big Indian (the sight of Rudi's Big Indian restaurant—if you're ever in the area and want a very special meal, make sure you go there!). We made a pilgrimage to Cooperstown to the Baseball Hall of Fame and for old time's sake drove through Woodstock, which was in process of celebrating the twentieth anniversary of the weekend that put it and the Woodstock generation on the map.

Evening found us tired, hungry, and passing through a one-wink-and-you-miss-it town called Bovina. On a gentle embankment off the side of the road sat the warm and welcoming yellow lights of a roadhouse. We pulled into the grassy area in front, lining up with pickups with deer rifles hung across the back windows, and stepped out of the car taking in the long, low-timbered building, the neon Bud sign, the cinder-block planters sporting marigolds, and a mellow (fortunately) Saint Bernard tied with a very thin rope to the front porch.

"This place is neat," exclaimed our six-year-old, letting the Saint Bernard's exuberant tongue remove all traces from his chin of the chocolate ice cream cone he had had for lunch. Patti Page crooned out the open door to the bar, which was in the front. While David and I stood on the porch deciding if we too thought this was a neat place, the chilly hand of early autumn pushed us through the initial hesitation and inside. Warm, moist, noisy air surrounded us as we followed an overall-clad woman to a table in the back. We passed farm families with tow-headed, freckled children out for Sunday supper and weary hunters up since way before sunrise, clad in the expected red-and-black-checked woolen shirts and hats discussing the day's bag, hunched heavily over a mug of steaming coffee or glass of beer.

There was a wonderful smell coming from the kitchen that the waitress told us was fried chicken—"specialty of the house." I was so hungry I could have eaten one of the pickup trucks parked in the front so fried chicken sounded just fine.

The jukebox blasted back and forth between Willie Nelson and Julio Iglesias. The waitress brought us Cokes in frosty old-fashioned sea green bottles, and we sipped the icy soda through paper straws while we interrupted each others' best moments of the lovely day. David's stellar achievement was in Cooperstown, outpitching his middle son in the speed-monitored pitching booth. Max let his father bask in that glory while gently reminding him that the elder Brody's performance in the batting cage was a woefully different story. Sam's moment was seeing the world's rarest baseball card. For me it was remembering that I was in the delivery room at Mount Sinai hospital when everyone else my age was gathering at Woodstock.

Just when my stomach's rumblings threatened to tune out Willie Nelson's lament on the jukebox, the waitress arrived with two enormous platters piled high with steaming, deep gold fried chicken. These went in the center of the table and around them, family style, she placed dishes of mashed potatoes, green beans, biscuits, and finally a big bowl of gravy. The combination of crispy, crunchy skin and fall-off-the-bone-tender meat underneath was heavenly. We ate with our hands, dunking the pieces right into the gravy bowl, at first wrapping napkins around the pieces to keep from burning our fingers, blowing on each bite as we went. All conversation stopped and did not resume until everything was gone but one final drumstick. "Gee, it looks so lonely there," I said, "but I'm soooo full. I'll burst if I eat one more bite." No one else seemed to have any room either, so the poor old drumstick continued to sit there. The waitress came by to collect the dirty dishes and as she removed the last platter from the table, I snatched that drumstick. "Mom. . .you're going to be sorry. . ." scolded Max, wagging a cautionary finger in my face. "Yup, I probably will," I agreed. "You'll have to use a shoehorn to get me into the car."

After I helped the others finish their gingerbread and vanilla ice cream, we headed out into the dark night. On the porch I yanked Sam away from the Saint Bernard, who was after any stray dinner crumbs that might be lurking on his face. "Stick to dog food, pal, this stuff's too good for the likes of you."

We drove home cautiously on the lookout for deer that were too dumb to realize that this was the hunting season. The parsonage's lights were visible in the valley below from almost a half mile away. The autumn chill had invaded the house so we quickly got into several layers of sleepwear and went to bed. The kids slept downstairs in the parlor turned dormitory, and David and I slept on the second floor in a bedroom furnished with items from the house's original owners. I drifted off to sleep to the sound of country night noises; mice playing tag in the walls, scampering back and forth, back and forth; a very far distant rumbling of a long-distance eighteen wheeler whining and straining up the steep valley road; an occasional bump and metallic rattle as the raccoons and deer tried to get past the wire fence into Stuart's garden. Mostly there was silence—deep, velvety black silence that is the perfect finish after a day devoted to good fun and great food.

That silence lasted exactly six hours. At five o'clock the following morning in the middle of our deepest sleep, in one terrible and deafening movement our bed collapsed. The 150-year-old lateral supports underneath gave up the ghost, and the bed and its occupants took a sudden, jolting, crashing one-way trip to the floor. I was sure there had been an earthquake and began screaming hysterically. David, the calm one, knew what had happened and sat on top of me until I stopped shrieking. It took me a full five minutes to stop shaking, then I thought of the kids, who surely had thought something terrible had happened. I crawled out of the tangle of sheets and blankets and ran downstairs. Sam (the child who couldn't sleep if someone next door was locked in the basement listening to the radio) was sound asleep. Max, however, was sitting bolt upright in the bed, his sleeping bag pulled tight around his chin. "Did you hear that?!" I asked.

"Yup, sure did," was his laconic reply. "I sure didn't think Dad had it in him."

"Max, give us a break for Christ sake, it's five o'clock in the morning!"

"Yeah, but I thought you old guys got a late start and went into extra innings."

I turned to go upstairs to try to salvage what was left of my interrupted sleep time, not to mention my dignity, and he shot after me, "Told you not to have that last piece of fried chicken."

Skillet Fried Chicken

This recipe calls for somewhat less oil than the traditional ones.

1 whole chicken cut into
  8 pieces
Salt, black pepper to taste
1 cup flour
1 egg, beaten

½ cup milk, or ½ cup beer or
  white wine
2 cups unseasoned
  bread crumbs
¾ cup vegetable oil
  (approximately)

Rinse the chicken and use paper towels to blot off as much moisture as possible. Season with salt and pepper. Place the flour in a plastic bag and dredge the chicken pieces in it. Combine the egg and milk in a small bowl, dip the chicken into this mixture, and then coat with the bread crumbs, using your hands to press the crumbs onto the chicken.

Heat the oil very hot in a heavy-bottomed skillet, place the chicken skin side down, and fry on high heat for 5 minutes or until quite brown. Turn the pieces over and brown. Reduce the heat to low and continue cooking for about 30 minutes. Check for doneness by inserting a fork into each piece—the juices should run clear.

Serves 4–6

Oven-Fried Chicken

This delectable, easy recipe needs to be started the day before since the chicken needs to marinate for at least 12 hours. Great for a family supper or large gathering, this recipe may be doubled, tripled, or quadrupled.

1 medium-sized roasting
chicken, cut up into 8 pieces

FOR THE MARINADE

½ cup vegetable oil
¼ cup soy sauce
3 tablespoons toasted
  sesame seeds
1 tablespoon sesame oil (the
  mild, not the hot, type)

2 tablespoons white wine or
  dry vermouth
2 cloves garlic, peeled and
  halved
1 teaspoon chili powder
½ teaspoon ginger

FOR THE COATING

1½ cups cornflakes, crushed,
  or store-bought cornflake
  crumbs

Combine all the marinade ingredients well. Rinse the chicken pieces and dry with a paper towel. Place the chicken in a large, heavy-duty zip-lock bag and add the marinade. Refrigerate for at least 12 hours, turning several times to distribute the marinade.

Preheat the oven to 350 degrees with the rack in the center position. Line a heavy-duty baking sheet with foil. Place the cornflake crumbs in a bowl and roll each piece of chicken in the crumbs until it is well coated. Place the pieces on the prepared sheet and bake for 1 hour.

Serves 4–6

Oven-Barbecued Chicken

This is another version of the previous recipe. When it's too cold to get out the charcoal and cook outside, this indoor version will satisfy your craving for barbecue.

1 whole chicken cut up into
    8 pieces
1 large onion, thinly sliced
Salt and pepper to taste
Hot water
¼ cup soy sauce
¼ cup vegetable oil
½ teaspoon paprika
1 teaspoon chili powder
½ cup water

4 tablespoons red wine vinegar
2 tablespoons Worcestershire
    sauce
1 8-ounce bottle chili sauce
½ cup brown sugar
Rind of 3 lemons
½ cup lemon juice
2 medium onions, chopped
4 cloves garlic, chopped

Preheat the oven to 350 degrees with the rack in the lower third, but not bottom, position.

Place the chicken pieces, skin side up, on a foil-lined baking sheet with at least 1-inch sides. Scatter the thinly sliced onion on top. Sprinkle with salt and pepper. Add enough hot water to cover the bottom of the pan. Bake for ½ hour. Turn the chicken skin side down and bake for an additional ½ hour. Meanwhile, combine all the remaining ingredients to make the sauce. Turn the chicken skin side up. Pour off all but ¾ cup of the juice from the chicken and add to the sauce. Pour the sauce over the chicken and continue to bake, basting with the sauce frequently until very tender—about another ½ hour.

Serves 4–6

Mashed Potatoes

With the twin advent of those disgusting instant mashed potatoes and calorie counters, it seems like no one remembers how to make real mashed potatoes anymore. Well, throw away those ersatz flakes and toss out Pritikin, here comes the real thing! The potatoes are boiled with their skins on because my mother says that you get more vitamins that way.

4 medium-sized baking
   potatoes (preferably Idaho)
4 tablespoons butter or
   margarine, at room
   temperature, cut in pieces

½–⅔ cup heavy cream (optional)
Salt and freshly ground white
   pepper to taste
Paprika (optional)

Scrub the potatoes and quarter them, leaving the skins on. Place them in a 2-quart pan and cover them with water. Boil until tender—about 20 minutes. Drain off the water and slip off the skins, taking care to remove any black spots from the potatoes. Put the potatoes in a bowl, add the butter or margarine, and mash with a potato masher. Add the (optional) cream and continue to mash until the lumps are gone. Add salt and pepper to taste and sprinkle with the paprika if desired.

Serves 4

Baked Stuffed Potatoes

Another great favorite at our house, and one that is a little dressier than plain mashed potatoes, is baked stuffed potatoes.

Bake 4 large Idaho potatoes in a 350-degree oven for about an hour. Cool slightly, cut in half lengthwise, and scoop out the insides, transferring them to a bowl. Proceed as with the preceding recipe for mashed potatoes. Spoon the mashed potatoes back into the reserved skins, sprinkle with grated cheese or paprika, run them under the broiler until slightly browned, and then serve.

These may be made in the morning and reheated just before serving.

Serves 4

Baking Powder Biscuits

2 cups all-purpose flour,
measured after sifting
2½ teaspoons baking powder
1 teaspoon salt

⅓ cup solid vegetable
shortening (Crisco)
⅔ cup light cream
(approximately)

Preheat the oven to 425 degrees with the rack in the center position.

Place the sifted flour, the baking powder, and the salt in a sifter and sift into a mixing bowl. Cut in the shortening until the mixture resembles coarse meal. Use a fork to blend in the cream, adding just enough cream so that the dough is soft but not sticky.

Lightly flour the counter or wooden board and turn the dough out onto it. Knead briefly until the dough is smooth. Use your hands to pat the dough into a rough circle about ½ inch thick. Flour a drinking glass or round cookie cutter with a 2-inch opening and use it to cut out the biscuits. Place the biscuits on a heavy, ungreased baking sheet, 1 inch apart, and bake for 12–14 minutes or until golden brown. If you find the bottoms are getting too dark, place a second baking sheet under the first and bake for an additional minute or so. Cool on a rack or serve hot.

These biscuits are best eaten fresh; however, they can be reheated and/or frozen.

Makes about 16 biscuits

Raisin Gingerbread

⅔ cup dark brown sugar,
  firmly packed
⅔ cup molasses
⅔ cup boiling water
4 tablespoons sweet (unsalted)
  butter, cut into chunks
  and at room temperature
1 teaspoon baking soda

1 extra large egg, well beaten
½ cup raisins
1½ cups flour, measured
  after sifting
1 teaspoon cinnamon
1 teaspoon ginger
¼ teaspoon cloves
¼ cup candied ginger,
  finely chopped

Preheat the oven to 350 degrees with the rack in the center position. Butter and dust with flour a 9-inch square pan. By hand or in the bowl of an electric mixer set on slow speed, blend together the sugar, molasses, boiling water, and butter. While the mixture is still hot, add the baking soda, egg, and raisins.

Sift together the flour, cinnamon, ginger, and cloves. Add to the batter. Stir into the molasses mixture, add the candied ginger, and mix well, taking care not to incorporate too many air bubbles into the batter. Pour into the prepared pan and bake for 35–40 minutes or until a cake tester inserted in the middle comes out dry.

Cool slightly and serve with whipped cream or cool completely and frost with the following icing.

GINGER CREAM CHEESE ICING

4 tablespoons sweet (unsalted)
  butter at room temperature
4 ounces cream cheese at
  room temperature
1½ cups confectioners sugar,
  sifted after measuring

1 teaspoon vanilla
¼ cup candied ginger,
  finely chopped

Beat the butter and cream cheese together until smooth. Add the sugar, beating until smooth. Mix in the vanilla and candied ginger. Chill briefly before frosting the gingerbread.

Serves 8

Smooth Food

The first time I ever tasted grits Minnie Mouse was standing over my shoulder. I was forty-two years old and attending a Character Breakfast with my six-year-old son at the Polynesian Resort Hotel at Disney World in Orlando, Florida. The two thoughts foremost in my mind at that moment were: I wonder if the person wearing that getup sweats a lot, and why did it take me so long to taste something this good? The grits were surrounded by a pool of melted butter and dusted with a generous helping of powdered sugar. The neutral taste and the substantially filling texture made me think of the Cream of Wheat that my mother made on cold winter days. They glided down my throat with the same comfortable and welcome feeling that I find in those foods that I call "smooth foods."

Smooth foods constitute an enormous category of comfort dishes. They can be sweet, spicy, hot, cold, summer, winter, fancy, or plain. They are the foods that glide down when you're depressed and need some cheering up, when you're sick and need some nursing, when you're freezing cold and need some inner warmth, when you're bored and need some distraction, and when you're anxious and need some calming down. They are split pea soup, refried beans, mashed potatoes, creamed spinach, and baked acorn squash with orange juice and brown sugar. They include all manner of things listed in the "forbidden" column in Weight Watchers: smoked salmon mousse, chicken liver paté with sherry, guacamole, sour cream, whipped cream, cream cheese, hommus, and every conceivable kind of cheese spread. Aside from grits they are oatmeal made from scratch, Wheatena, and Maypo—served piping hot with a substantial amount of butter, cream, and brown sugar. They encompass the whole spectrum of puddings: chocolate pudding, vanilla and butterscotch pudding, tapioca, rice, Grape-Nut, and bread puddings. They are baked custards—especially crème brûlée. They are Jell-O, yogurt, creamy peanut butter eaten right out of the jar, and my mother's homemade blackberry jam.

I would be remiss if I did not include in this list things like frosting roses from on top of store-bought birthday cakes, Junior Mints and melted Hershey's Kisses, penuche fudge, and halvah.

Proust's nostalgic rush with his madeleine was no match for the flood of smooth foods that came rushing to my mind when I ate those grits in Orlando.

Indian Pudding

¾ cup yellow cornmeal
1 quart whole milk
4 tablespoons sweet (unsalted)
 butter, melted
½ cup molasses
1 teaspoon salt
2 teaspoons cinnamon

1 teaspoon ginger
2 tablespoons amaretto
 (optional)
3 extra large eggs
⅓ cup dark brown sugar,
 firmly packed
Vanilla ice cream

Preheat the oven to 350 degrees with the rack in the lower third, but not lowest, position. Butter a 1½-quart ovenproof glass baking dish (a soufflé dish is good for this).

Place the cornmeal in the top of a double boiler set over hot water. Scald the milk and slowly stir it into the cornmeal. Place the double boiler over medium heat and cook the cornmeal until it starts to thicken and resembles a creamy hot cereal.

In a large bowl mix together the butter, molasses, salt, cinnamon, ginger, and optional amaretto. Beat in the eggs and sugar. Add the thickened cornmeal and mix well. Pour into prepared baking dish and place the dish in a larger pan with at least 2-inch sides. Place both pans in the oven and fill the larger pan with 1 inch of hot water. Bake for 1 hour.

Serve hot with a scoop of vanilla ice cream.

Serves 8

Creamy Rice Pudding

½ cup uncooked white rice—
not instant cooking
3 cups whole milk
½ teaspoon salt
3 tablespoons sweet (unsalted)
butter
3 extra large eggs,
lightly beaten

1 cup granulated sugar
1 cup light cream
1 teaspoon vanilla
½ cup raisins
Nutmeg and cinnamon to
taste

Preheat the oven to 350 degrees with the rack in the center position. Butter a shallow rectangular Pyrex pan or 2-quart casserole and set aside. Combine the rice, 2 cups of milk, and the salt and cook over low heat stirring occasionally until the rice is tender—approximately 20 minutes. Stir in the butter, stirring until it melts. Whisk together the eggs and sugar, then add this to the rice mixture. Heat the remaining milk plus the light cream to just below scalding and pour this into the rice mixture. Mix in the vanilla. Mix well to combine all the ingredients, smoothing any lumps in the rice. Stir in the raisins.

Pour into the prepared pan and sprinkle lightly with nutmeg and cinnamon. Bake for 45–50 minutes or until the top is golden and the middle is set. Take care not to overbake because you will lose the creamy consistency.

Chill or serve at room temperature with a garnish of whipped cream, if desired.

Serves 10–12

Baked Acorn Squash

4 acorn squashes of roughly
    similiar size
8 tablespoons butter
8 tablespoons brown sugar

Juice and finely grated rind of
    3 large oranges
2 teaspoons nutmeg
Salt and pepper to taste

Preheat the oven to 350 degrees with the rack in the center position. Line a heavy-duty baking sheet or large shallow pan with foil. Use a heavy chef's knife or serrated knife to cut each squash in half and remove the seeds. Place in the well of each squash half 1 tablespoon of butter and 1 tablespoon of brown sugar. Divide the orange juice and rind between each half. Sprinkle each with ¼ teaspoon of nutmeg. Bake for 1 hour or until very tender.

Serves 8

Hommus

This recipe makes a quart of hommus, which is enough for a large cocktail party or to satisfy the crowd watching the football game. It will keep for several weeks in the refrigerator, or you can cut the recipe in half.

4 large cloves of garlic, peeled and very finely minced

2 10-ounce cans chick-peas, drained of their liquid

1 cup tahini (sesame paste) available in specialty stores and Middle Eastern food markets

1 cup water

½ cup vegetable oil

Strained juice of 4 lemons

2 teaspoons salt

1 teaspoon white pepper

½ teaspoon cayenne pepper

2 teaspoons ground cumin

In the work bowl of a food processor or blender, process the garlic (which should be finely chopped first by hand), the chickpeas, tahini, water, oil, and half the lemon juice. Process until very smooth, adding a little more water if the mixture is very thick (it should be the consistency of a smooth, soft vegetable puree). Add the salt, white pepper, cayenne, cumin, and the rest of the lemon juice to taste. Add more salt and pepper if necessary.

Refrigerate well before serving with triangles of pita bread.

Makes 1 quart

Sam's Guacamole

My grand buddy Sam Arnold serves this famous genuine Old Mexico recipe in his restaurant, The Fort, in Morrison, Colorado. Stop by and enjoy some there or make it at home and drink a toast to Sam.

4 ripe avocados, peeled and
  diced (½-inch squares)
1 medium onion, finely
  chopped
2 medium-sized flavorful
  tomatoes, finely chopped
Leaves from 4 sprigs fresh
  cilantro (coriander),
  cut in half

4 fresh serrano chilies
  (available in specialty stores),
  finely minced
Juice of 1 large or 2 medium-
  sized limes
½ teaspoon salt or to taste

Mix all the ingredients together leaving avocados lumpy. Serve with corn chips and gusto.

Serves 8–10

Grape-Nut Pudding

4 extra large eggs
1 cup sugar
4 cups whole milk
½ cup currants
1 teaspoon vanilla

½ teaspoon salt
6–7 tablespoons Grape-Nuts
1 tablespoon sugar mixed
   with ½ teaspoon cinnamon
   and ½ teaspoon nutmeg

Preheat the oven to 350 degrees with the rack in the center position. Butter a 1½-quart ovenproof baking dish.

In the bowl of an electric mixer beat the eggs and sugar until the mixture is thick and pale yellow. Scald the milk and add it to the egg mixture. Add the currants, vanilla, and salt. Pour into the prepared pan and then sprinkle in the Grape Nuts. Dust with the cinnamon/nutmeg sugar. Bake for 55–60 minutes or until the center is firm and a cake tester comes out dry.

Serve warm or at room temperature with whipped cream.

Serves 6–8

Crème Brûlée

---

5 cups heavy cream
8 extra large egg yolks
½ cup plus 2 tablespoons
  granulated sugar

2 teaspoons vanilla extract
2–3 tablespoons boiling water
1⅓ cups dark brown sugar,
  firmly packed

Preheat the oven to 350 degrees and place the rack in the lower, but not lowest, position of the oven. Set 8 1-cup ovenproof custard cups or ramekins into a shallow roasting pan or jelly roll pan with at least 1-inch sides. The cups should not touch.

Scald the cream in a heavy-bottomed saucepan. Beat the egg yolks and sugar together in a large bowl and slowly dribble in the hot cream. Stir in the vanilla and strain the custard into another bowl.

Divide the custard among the 8 cups and place them in the oven, adding about 1 inch of hot water to the pan they sit in. Bake 35–40 minutes or just until the custard is set but still soft in the middle. When cooked, refrigerate the custard very well.

Set the broiler on high with the rack in the upper postion. Mix the boiling water and brown sugar together to make a thick paste. Use the back of a small spoon to spread about 2 table-spoons of the mixture on top of each custard. Set the cups on a cookie sheet and broil until the sugar bubbles and starts to get very brown. Refrigerate again until serving time.

Serves 8

Creamed Spinach
with Toasted Pine Nuts

Perhaps spinach wasn't your favorite vegetable when you were a kid. Well, you're grown-up now, and this version of Popeye's magic food is waiting to change your mind.

20 ounces fresh spinach, rinsed very well	4 tablespoons heavy cream
	½ teaspoon nutmeg
1 cup chicken stock or 1 cup boiling water and ½ cube Knorr's chicken bouillon	1 tablespoon soy sauce
	Salt and pepper to taste
	⅔ cup pine nuts
4 tablespoons butter	2 tablespoons butter

Remove the stems from the spinach and place it in a large pot or kettle. Add the stock or water and bouillon, cover the pot, and cook for about 5 minutes—only until the spinach is wilted. Drain off the liquid and reserve about ½ cup. Place the spinach in the work bowl of a food processor and puree. Add the butter, and when it has melted add the cream and the seasonings and soy sauce. If you like the puree looser, add some of the cooking liquid, a little bit at a time. Remove the puree to a bowl.

Sauté the pine nuts in the butter and stir into the spinach. Serve hot.

Serves 6

The World's Most
Delicious Chocolate Pudding

That's no modest claim. Well, this is not your usual chocolate pudding. Better hide an extra dish of it in the back of refrigerator because this will go so fast there might not be any left for the cook.

4 extra large egg yolks
¾ cup sugar
4 tablespoons all purpose flour
1 ounce (3 tablespoons)
   cornstarch
2½ cups whole milk

5 ounces semisweet chocolate,
   chopped
2 ounces unsweetened
   chocolate, chopped
1 teaspoon vanilla extract
Heavy cream (for garnish)

In a medium-sized bowl mix the egg yolks, sugar, flour, and cornstarch, adding 1 or 2 tablespoons of milk to make a smooth paste.

Scald the remaining milk and add it to the egg/flour mixture. Place this mixture in a saucepan and whisk constantly over medium heat until it begins to boil and thicken. Lower the heat and cook for 2 more minutes. Take care not to let the bottom burn. Off the heat add both chocolates and the vanilla and stir until the chocolate melts and the mixture is smooth.

Pour into individual glasses and cool first at room temperature and then refrigerate until serving time.

Serve with a thin layer of heavy cream on top.

Serves 6–8

Gourmet Chicken Soup?

The week before Passover last year I had major surgery and a long hospital stay, so for the first time in my adult life I had to delegate all of the cooking responsibility to friends and family. This was not easy for me to do, since one of the things that perpetuates my delusions about being young, energetic, and totally in control of my life is that every year I pull off a multicourse Seder for at least twenty all by myself. Every year my guests call to ask what can they do, what can they bring, and in the past I said, "Just bring yourselves." This year it was about all I could do to wander downstairs in my bathrobe and slippers and stay upright at the table for the meal.

The hardest thing for me to delegate was the chicken soup. I take inordinate pride in my version of this treasured classic and, as a matter of fact, I think (with all due modesty) that it's about the best there is. The recipe is a compilation of formulas of chicken soups I have revered; from my days as a restaurant cook I take the light, flavorful homemade chicken stock, from my mother-in-law I take chunks of carrot and parsnip and a sprinkling of dill. From my aunts Rose and Sarah I leave a little fat (for extra flavor) glistening on top and a generous sprinkling of pepper, and from my mother I take the recipe for the world's best matzo balls. When I was first married and thought I knew it all, I used a matzo ball recipe from the back of some box, and the results were something that my husband suggested sending to Israel for ammunition.

My good friend the wine maven generously offered to bring the soup. How could I say no? He is a wonderful cook, with a continental flair born of many, many trips to the first-class food captials of the world. I figured if anyone knew chicken soup he would. "Don't forget the balls," I reminded him at the end of the conversation.

The day came and our guests arrived bearing foil-covered trays, pans, and plates. It was rumored that my dear friend and cook extraordinaire, Irene Pletka, had come bearing her famous lemon Passover tart and a plum terrine. I lay in bed upstairs feeling well loved and not a little relieved at missing the commotion as the guests took over the kitchen. Soon I was summoned to take my place at the table. During the Seder I looked down the length of the table at my family and friends, their faces caught in the golden glow of the candles, and thanked the powers that be for letting me greet this, my favorite holiday and my favorite season, in good health and high spirits and in the company of people I dearly loved.

The gefilte fish (homemade!) was silky smooth, and my tongue was set ablaze with my mother's horseradish. The sweet, thick ruby red Passover wine quelled the fire.

Next came the soup. I couldn't wait. In fact, I didn't wait—I wandered into the kitchen (amidst great shouts of "Sit down or go back to bed!" from my mother and husband) just to peek into the pot on the stove. I lifted the lid and bent over to inhale the Jewish ambrosia. I hesitated. I had never seen brown chicken soup before. And it was perfectly clear. The smell was unbelievably rich—like a double consommé. The soup maker was beaming with pride. "I used eight chickens to make it!" he told me. "Then I simmered it until it was reduced by half and clarified it so it would be crystal clear without any traces of fat. It's the richest stock I've ever made."

"Escoffier would be proud," said my mother, who shared my view of the way chicken soup should be. She meant Escoffier wasn't Jewish and neither is this soup.

"Where are the matzo balls?" I asked, looking around at the other pots on the stove. I got a look of I-give-you-diamonds-and-you-want-to-know-where-the-rubies-are and a reply of, "It was so much work to make the damn soup, I didn't have time for the matzo balls." Maybe you think I'm way out of line, but to me Passover with highfalutin' chicken soup and no matzo balls is unnatural—sort of akin to a pastrami sandwich on a croissant.

The soup was unquestionably delicious—heart-stoppingly rich and dramatically aromatic and seriously gourmet. But it wasn't chicken soup. Out loud I praised my friend's efforts and thanked him profusely. Silently I thanked God for giving me next year so that I could make the soup. . .and the balls.

Chicken Soup

Making chicken soup is not like the exact science of baking a cake or making a soufflé in that the soup recipe is structured so there is plenty of leeway for incorporating your own taste preferences. Feel free to experiment with the addition of your favorite root vegetables and herbs. Take care, though, not to overpower the taste of the chicken.

I buy pullets in a kosher meat market. If you can't find them the next best thing is a fowl (a chicken that is killed when it is older, larger, and more flavorful than a young one). Lacking both these things use twice the amount of a regular fryer.

2 pullets or 1 large fowl
Several packages of chicken
  necks and backs
2 cubes Knorr's chicken
  bouillon
3 large onions, peeled and
  sliced
4 carrots, cut into
  2-inch chunks
3 parsnips, cut into
  2-inch chunks
4 stalks of celery, leaves
  included, cut into 2-inch
  slices

1 bunch parsley, well rinsed
2 teaspoons black peppercorns
5 cloves of garlic, peeled
Approximately 3–4 quarts of
  cold water
Salt and freshly ground black
  pepper to taste
Additional chunks of carrots,
  celery, parsnip, and sliced
  onion
Fresh dill sprigs

Rinse the chicken and necks and backs well and place them in a very large pot or kettle. Add the bouillon cubes and the cut-up vegetables, parsley, peppercorns, and garlic. Cover completely with cold water and bring to a simmer. Cover the pot, leaving the lid off center so that some steam escapes.

Cook for 2 hours on very low heat—the soup should be just barely simmering. Let the soup cool with the chicken in it for 1 additional hour, and then strain off the liquid. You should have about 3 quarts of liquid.

Refrigerate until very cold and then scrape off the fat, which will have solidified on top. The fat can be used for the matzo balls or to make chopped liver. It will freeze beautifully in a covered plastic container. You can use the stewed chicken for chicken salad or add it back to the soup before serving (it won't have much taste). Discard the cooked vegetables (or eat them out of the bottom of the pot the way I do).

Reheat the soup and taste before adding any additional vegetables or seasoning. If the soup is very undersalted, I like to add another bouillon cube rather than straight salt; if you do this try adding ½ a cube at a time to avoid oversalting. I like lots of pepper in my soup. Add the remaining vegetables and cook only until they are tender. Serve with matzo balls if desired (recipe follows), and sprigs of fresh dill.

Makes about 3 quarts of soup

Matzo Balls I

---

*Can you imagine that there are some people who think that matzo
balls are only for Passover? Matzo meal is available other months of
the year, and matzo balls are as delicious in July as they are in February.*

1 medium onion, finely diced
5 tablespoons rendered
　chicken fat (skimmed off
　the top of the cooled
　chicken soup)
4 eggs
1 cup matzo meal
4 tablespoons seltzer
　(sparkling water)

⅓ cup fresh parsely, minced
⅓ cup fresh dill, chopped, or
　2 teaspoons dried dill
2 teaspoons salt
Freshly ground pepper to taste
3 quarts water
3 chicken bouillon cubes
　(I prefer Knorr's)

Sauté the onions in the chicken fat. Place the eggs in a 2-quart
bowl and use a fork to beat them lightly. Stir in the onions and
chicken fat. Stir in the matzo meal, the sparkling water, the
parsley, and the seasonings. Cover the bowl and refrigerate for
½ hour.

Bring the water to a boil and add the bouillon cubes. Reduce
the heat and with the water lightly bubbling use a wet tablespoon
and your hand (it's easier if you moisten your hand with a little
cold water) to form walnut-sized balls. Drop them into the soup
as they are formed. Cover the pot and cook 35 minutes. If you
are making the matzo balls ahead, let them cool for 15 minutes
in the cooking liquid before transferring them to a bowl with
a slotted spoon; if not, transfer them to soup bowls and add hot
chicken soup.

Makes about 18–20 matzo balls

Matzo Balls II

This version takes a bit more time because you have to separate the eggs and beat the whites, folding them into the matzo meal mixture. The result is a lighter matzo ball.

1 medium onion, very finely diced	2 teaspoons salt
3 tablespoons chicken fat	Freshly ground black pepper to taste
8 eggs, separated and at room temperature	½ cup minced dill
	1½ cups matzo meal

Sauté the onion in the chicken fat. Beat the egg yolks until they form a thick ribbon when the beater is lifted from the bowl, and then beat in the salt, pepper, and dill. Beat the egg whites until they hold soft peaks, and fold ¼ of the whites into the yolks. Sift half the meal on top of the egg mixture and gently fold in. Fold in the remaining whites, sift the remaining meal over the egg mixture, and gently fold together so that no dry meal is visible. Refrigerate, covered, for 1 hour.

Bring 4 quarts of salted water or soup to a gentle simmer. Use a wet soupspoon to form walnut-sized balls and add them to the cooking liquid. Cook, covered, at a gentle simmer for 30 minutes. Do not lift the pot's lid until 20 minutes have passed.

Makes about 30 matzo balls

Gefilte Fish

This is a big job but, of course, worth it. You must have access to really fresh whitefish, pike, and carp. In this recipe, I'm afraid, there can be no substitutions.

1⅔ pounds whitefish fillets
1⅔ pounds pike fillets
1⅔ pounds carp fillets
The frames from the above
    fish, without gills (to reserve
    for fish cooking liquid)
2 large onions, finely chopped

2 extra large eggs,
    slightly beaten
2 tablespoons matzo meal
1 teaspoon salt
1 teaspoon freshly ground
    black pepper
1 teaspoon sugar

Either have your fishmonger grind the fish twice, or grind it in the work bowl of a food processor fitted with the metal blade until very finely textured. Combine the fish, onions, and eggs. Mix well. Mix in the matzo meal, the salt, pepper, and sugar. Scoop out approximately 3 tablespoons of the mixture and use your hands to form a ball. Flatten slightly in the palm of your hand to form an oval shape. There should be enough filling for 1 dozen balls. Refrigerate while you prepare the fish cooking liquid.

FOR THE FISH COOKING LIQUID

Fish frames from fish
    used above
6 cups water
3 large carrots, peeled and
    sliced into ½-inch slices

2 onions, sliced
1 teaspoon salt
1 teaspoon pepper
1 teaspoon sugar

Place all the ingredients in a large kettle or Dutch oven and bring to a boil. Lower the heat and simmer, uncovered, for 30 minutes. Place the fish balls in the pot with a slotted spoon, cover, and simmer for 1½ hours. Use a slotted spoon to remove the gefilte fish from the pot and then strain the remaining liquid, making sure all the fish bones are removed. Reserve the carrot slices. Combine the strained liquid and the carrots with the fish and chill very well—for at least 8 hours before serving. Serve with horseradish sauce on page 198.

Makes 1 dozen gefilte fish

Horseradish

Don't make the mistake of sticking your nose close to the bowl to inhale the aroma—your face will feel like it's going to explode! Serve small amounts—this is powerful stuff. It makes store-bought gefilte fish taste like homemade.

1 fresh horseradish root, trimmed and peeled	1 beet, either freshly cooked or canned Red wine vinegar

Either grate the horseradish root by hand or cut it into small chunks and process in a food processor fitted with a steel blade until ground but not pureed—an on-and-off motion a few seconds at a time is the best way to achieve the proper consistency. Grate the beet and add it to the horseradish, or remove the horseradish from the food processor, chop the beet the same way, and combine the two in a small bowl. Store the horseradish in a glass jar with a screw cap, cover the top with vinegar, and refrigerate. Serve with gefilte fish.

Irene Pletka's Dragonfly Tart
(Lemon Curd Passover Tart)

FOR THE CRUST

¾ cup blanched almonds
1½ sticks (6 ounces) sweet
   (unsalted) butter
1 cup granulated sugar
1 cup matzo meal

1 teaspoon cinnamon
½ teaspoon cloves
Rind of one lemon,
   finely grated
1 extra large egg

In the work bowl of a food processor fitted with the steel blade, finely grind the almonds. Set them aside and place the butter and sugar in the food processor and process until well blended. Add the meal, cinnamon, and cloves to the butter and sugar in the food processor and process until smooth. Add the lemon rind, almonds, and egg to the mixture in the food processor and process until the batter forms a ball. Wrap the dough in plastic wrap and chill for at least 30 minutes.

FOR THE LEMON CURD FILLING

7 egg yolks
1 cup sugar
1 stick sweet (unsalted) butter
Rind of 2 lemons, finely grated

¼ cup lemon juice (or more—
   depending on how tart you
   like the curd)

In the top of a double boiler set over gently simmering water, combine all the ingredients and stir until the curd starts to thicken. Immediately strain into another bowl. Add more lemon juice if desired.

TO ASSEMBLE AND GARNISH

Crystallized violets
2 small dried apricots

Preheat the oven to 350 degrees with the rack in the center position. Butter or use Crisco to grease a 9-inch or 10-inch springform pan. Use your fingers and press a thin layer of about ½ to ⅔ of dough on the bottom. Bake for 10 minutes or until lightly colored. Meanwhile, roll the remaining dough into thin (pencil width) strips and set aside. Cool the baked shell for 20 minutes—or long enough so that you can very comfortably touch the pan. Place the strips of dough around the base of the crust and press them 1–1½ inches up the sides of the pan. Chill for 15 minutes.

Spoon the lemon curd into the shell and bake in a 350-degree oven for about 45 minutes or until the sides and the curd is well set.

As soon as the tart comes out of the oven place a crystallized violet in the center. With luck, the coloring will run slightly, creating the dragonfly body. Snip the 2 apricots in half and arrange them around the violet as wings. Chill the tart for at least 6–8 hours before serving.

Serves 8–10

The Velveeta Cook-Off

I guess I must have a pretty solid ego when it comes to taste (I mean that literally—as in the taste of food) because it didn't bother me a bit when my upscale cooking cronies guffawed and rolled their eyes when I announced that I was going to Chicago to be a judge in the Velveeta Creative Cooking Contest. "Velveeta!" they screamed in horrified chorus, elbowing each other as if I had served up a fallen soufflé. "We wouldn't be caught dead eating something that has the shelf life of the World Book Encyclopedia and the personality of third year calculus."

Funny thing was, though, that one by one when they phoned me to try to figure out why I was really doing this (money? fame? Robert Redford was the other judge?), they each admitted to a certain weakness for some dish from their childhoods made with Velveeta. For one it was a special casserole, another waxed rhapsodic about some strange-sounding concoction featuring Velveeta and costarring an unlikely cast of canned onion rings and frozen green beans (and perhaps cranberries?). Mercifully, I think I blocked the rest of the ingredients. My hypocritical phone-ins got so carried away by their recollections that they lost interest in why I was doing it. I had no loving childhood attachments to Velveeta. As a matter of fact, I had never even tasted Velveeta. The truth was that my friend Karen Slater (the maker of Christmas cookies on page 167) lived in Chicago, and I would eat library paste in exchange for a chance to see her. Velveeta sounded great by comparison.

I told the nice people at Velveeta I would be glad to eat as much cheese as they dished out if they would (1) let me take the train to Chicago (I hate to fly and will do so only in emergencies or if the plane is going to Paris) and (2) if I could bring my son Sam, then seven years old. I figured Sam would enjoy a trip to Chicago and would be great company on the train. The answer from cheeseland was a cheerful "yes."

Since I spend lots of time on trains and know that cooking by Amtrak can put a damper on your trip, Sam and I traveled prepared. We packed a hamper of delicious things to eat: tender, sweet dried apricots, giant cashews, Ritz crackers smeared with chunky peanut butter from the health food store, crisp Golden Delicious apples, juicy red grapes, oatmeal-raisin cookies, and bottles of fruit juice. That was the healthy stuff. For junk food we had laid in a supply of beer nuts, M and M's (plain and peanut), milk chocolate Toblerone, Cape Cod potato chips, root beer barrels for me, and Pez for Sam.

We boarded the "sleeping train" (as Sam called it) in Boston and found our compartment. Immediately a young porter with an exotic accent peeked in to show us how to work the knobs and switches that controlled the lights, fan, and call buttons. We made ourselves at home on the couches while he hoisted our baggage onto the racks above. He said he'd be back after supper to make our beds.

The train pulled out of South Station on its twenty-hour journey across Massachusetts, northern New York (Buffalo and the Erie Canal), west across Pennsylvania, Ohio, and finally Illinois. The early May light lasted a long time, and Sam and I watched the rapidly moving panorama of freight yards turning into forests becoming backyards filled with aboveground pools in some places and chicken coops in others. Farms and fields flew by as twilight made it difficult to pick out signposts that would tell us which town we were traveling through.

Our porter reappeared with a basket of cheese and crackers and a bottle of wine for me. This was Amtrak? He asked which seating we would like for dinner. We chose the early one and while we were not blown away by the quality of the food, neither were we insulted. "Mom, does Velveeta taste like this?" Sam wanted to know. "I hope not," was my answer. We ate lightly, knowing that back in our compartment a true feast waited.

We wove our way back toward the sleeping car and found the porter making up the bunk beds. Sam asked him about hoboes— had he ever seen any. Not many here in the States, he said, but in Poland, where he came from, there were many hoboes who rode the rails during the day and made camp fires near the tracks at night. Sam was determined to stay up all night and watch for hoboes from his lookout on the upper bunk.

We ate our picnic on the lower bunk, spreading the goodies on top of my blanket. Lights flashed and streamed by in the blackness outside as we sped on too fast to read the signs of stations in towns too small for this train to stop. Sam made a detailed exploration of our compartment, figuring out that he could jump from the top of the toilet seat to the top bunk and back again without breaking his front teeth. I got into bed and invited him to snuggle with me with the promise that we could see outside better if we turned out the lights. We munched on Toblerones and Sam wanted to know, ''Is Velveeta as good as this?'' ''Probably not,'' I answered.

We sang all the railroad songs we could think of: ''I've Been Working on the Railroad,'' ''Peace Train,'' ''Freight Train,'' ''500 Miles,'' ''Chattanooga Choo Choo,'' ''Take the 'A' Train,'' ''Hobo's Lullaby.'' Were there hoboes huddled out there in the blackness? Sam swears he saw them. I found it impossible to resist the soothing rocking of the train, and in spite of the potato chip crumbs between my sheets I fell right to sleep.

We pulled into Chicago's Union Station and tumbled out of the train to face a uniformed man holding a sign with my name on it. Sam and I exchanged a look, shrugged, and followed his lead through the station and out to the street where a long black limousine stood waiting. The driver opened the door and inclined his head toward us. Sam's eyes bugged out in his head. For once in his short life he was speechless. As the limo pulled away from the curb, Sam came to and gave the interior a thorough going-over—figuring out how to work the TV, the intercom, and the telephone. Then he sat back in the smooth leather seat, his short legs dangling off the floor, and sighed contentedly.

''Sam,'' I said, ''who do you think the people outside think is riding in this limousine?''

''President Sam,'' he answered matter-of-factly.

The suite that was reserved for us at the Ritz was as luxurious and extravagant as our transportation to it. There was a view of Lake Michigan that made us feel as if we were standing at the prow of a stately yacht. I kept reminding myself that no matter how hard it was going to be to eat all that Velveeta, it was worth it.

That evening Sam and I were joined by my friend Karen and three of her children in the dining room at the Ritz. The waiter hovered over us, bringing heavenly things to eat and drink. When Sam's eyes grew heavy (from sitting up all night looking for hoboes), he put his head down on my lap and went to sleep. The waiter drew another chair close and gently put Sam's legs up and covered him up with a clean tablecloth. When he awoke the waiter presented him with a miniature pastry basket filled with tiny balls of chocolate ice cream. As the waiter poured chocolate sauce from a silver pitcher over his dessert, Sam rubbed the sleep from his eyes and murmured, "Mom, I know Velveeta isn't as good as this. . . ."

We went to sleep in the king-sized bed next to the window overlooking the twinkling lights of boats on Lake Michigan and, facing the next day of thirty-five dishes made with Velveeta, I sat up for a while thinking about what I had gotten myself into. Memories of culinary ecstasy rumbled in my stomach, and I resigned myself to an episode of gustatory good news, bad news.

The next morning Sam set off to the zoo with a baby-sitter from the hotel, and I headed over to a downtown restaurant where the other judges were gathering for the contest. I was pleasantly surprised by the attractive and elaborate setup the people running the contest had constructed. There were five categories of recipes: soups, egg dishes, vegetables, main courses, and snacks. Each category had its own station, and each station was beautifully decorated with pretty dishes, tableware, and flowers. The six judges (all cooks or food writers like me) sat at a long table, and the dishes were first presented to us for aesthetic scrutiny and then we tasted.

As each caldron of soup was brought out, I was astonished at the wonderful aroma emanating from the pots. I could tell the other judges were impressed, too. I think we were all relieved that this experience stood to be a lot more pleasant than we had all anticipated. We tasted six soups in all. I could not believe how delicious the first one was. It was a light and delicately creamy soup filled to overflowing with tender, yet slightly crunchy, vegetables and backed by a subtle but hearty cheese taste. I had a hard time restraining myself from eating the whole bowl—but

I knew that if I didn't save room for the next thirty-four courses I would be dead meat in the eyes of the Kraft Corporation. The next soup was almost as good—as were the other four.

The next categories were just as interesting and in some cases just as delicious. I began to wonder if Velveeta was different when my friends back home were growing up—or perhaps their mothers were just lousy cooks. The dishes I was eating that day were really very good. With all due honesty, there were a few clunkers—but nothing outright terrible—and those few were definitely balanced by the dishes that were superb. Now we are not talking haute cuisine, but we are talking down-home good taste, pleasing texture, and in many cases stunning presentation.

When the last category rolled around I was rolling too. I had had seconds of almost everything, and I was hard-pressed to pick a winner. There was an apple snack cake that was fantastic. Some judges thought that it didn't have enough cheese in it to make it a real Velveeta dish—but everyone thought that the taste was tops.

In the end, the vegetable soup—which we all agreed was special—got the first prize. And we all agreed that our perceptions of Velveeta had been changed or, in some cases, updated. When I picked Sam up at the hotel, I was happy to report to him that the Velveeta dishes were really good . . . almost as good as his chocolate ice cream at the Ritz.

Macaroni and cheese made with Velveeta has become a staple at our house. My family loves it. One night when I have my fancy food friends over I think I'll serve it under an assumed name and take pleasure watching them gobble it up.

Italian Harvest Soup

---

1 cup chicken stock or
  1 chicken bouillon cube
  dissolved in 1 cup hot water,
  or 1 cup meatless vegetable
  stock
1 small onion, chopped
¾ cup zucchini, cut in
  ½-inch pieces
½ cup carrots, cut in
  ½-inch pieces
1 red pepper, coarsely
  chopped

1 teaspoon dried oregano
1 teaspoon dried basil
¼ teaspoon red pepper flakes
1 8-ounce package Velveeta,
  cut in 1-inch cubes
2½ cups milk
1 tablespoon butter
1 tablespoon flour
Salt and pepper to taste
Garlic croutons (recipe follows)
Grated parmesan cheese

Place the chicken stock, vegetables, and seasonings in a skillet, bring the liquid to a boil, lower the heat, cover and cook for about 15 minutes or just until the vegetables are tender.

Meanwhile, heat the milk and add the Velveeta, stirring until the Velveeta melts. Place the butter and flour together in a small pan and cook over low heat, stirring constantly for two minutes. Whisk this into the hot milk and cook over low heat, stirring constantly until the mixture thickens slightly. Add the vegetables and their liquid. Season with salt and pepper, sprinkle with garlic croutons and grated cheese and serve.

GARLIC CROUTONS

4 slices thick cut whole grain
  bread (this recipe works better
  if the bread is slightly stale)

1 clove garlic, peeled
  and chopped
3 tablespoons olive oil
Salt and pepper to taste

These can be made ahead and stored in a covered plastic container. Cut the bread into ½-inch cubes. Heat the oil, add the garlic, and cook over low heat for a few minutes, until the garlic just begins to brown. Use a slotted spoon to remove the garlic. Sauté the bread cubes in the oil (adding more if necessary) until they are browned and crisp. Season with salt and pepper to taste and drain on paper towels.

Serves 4

Glossary

Definitions of Jewish Terms
(the gospel according to our family)

Babka: yeasted sweet bread, often made with nuts and raisins.

Bar Mitzvah: ceremony (usually during the Saturday morning synagogue service) in which a thirteen-year-old boy is called to the Torah (sacred scroll containing the Five Books of Moses) and assumes adult status in the eyes of the community.

Blintzes: cheese- or fruit-filled crepes that are sautéed and served with sour cream.

Bris: ritual circumcision.

Bubbe: Jewish grandmother.

Challa: braided egg bread.

Chachke: (also spelled Tsatske) a toy, plaything.

Chanukah: the December Festival of Lights, commemorating the Maccabees' (Jewish soldiers) victory over Syrian soldiers in 167 B.C.

Dreidel: spinning top used at Chanukah.

Gefilte fish: ground poached fish balls (tastes better than this sounds).

Haftorah: a chapter from the books of Prophets read in the synagogue on the Sabbath and holidays.

Halvah: candy made from ground sesame seeds and honey.

Judah Maccabee: the leader of the Maccabees, whose courage is remembered at Chanukah.

Kaddish: the mourner's prayer.

Kasha varnishkes: a savory mixture of roasted buckwheat and noodles.

Kosher: conforming to Jewish dietary rules.

Kuchen: a baked dessert usually made with fruit and a crumb topping. Also a yeasted sweet cake.

Kugel: a baked pudding made with either noodles or potatoes.

Maccabees: see Chanukah.

Matzo: unleavened bread.

Matzo ball soup: chicken soup served with dumplings made from ground matzos.

Menorah: candelabrum used during Chanukah.

Mohel: rabbi (or doctor) who performs ritual circumcisions.

Oy!: exclamation for all occasions, usually said while hitting your forehead with the palm of your hand.

Passover: eight-day celebration of freedom recalling when Moses led the Jews out of Egypt.

Potato latkes: pancakes traditionally served during Chanukah.

Purim: spring holiday commemorating Queen Esther, who short-circuited a plot by the wicked Haman to kill the Jews of Persia.

Rabbi: teacher.

Rosh Hashana: the Jewish New Year.

Rugelach: small, buttery crescent cookies filled with nuts and raisins.

Seder: ceremony and meal held during Passover.

Shmate: a rag.

Shmaltzy: corny.

Shul: synagogue.

Sissle: caraway, as in sissle rye bread.

Sitting shiva: observing the week of mourning for the dead.

Trayf: not kosher.

Yizkor: a memorial service.

Yortzeit: anniversary of a death.

Zayde: Jewish grandfather.

Index

Acorn Squash, Baked, 184
American cheese, in
  Grilled Cheese
    Sandwich, 62
Apple(s). *See also*
  Applesauce
  in Herring Salad, 8
  in Honey Cake I, 141
  in Honey Cake II, 142
  Pie, Deep-Dish, 56
  Strudel, 117–18
  in Waldorf Salad, 156
Applesauce, 90
  Raspberry, 91
Apricot(s)
  as dragonfly (lemon
    curd) tart garnish,
    199–200
  Jell-O Mold, 128–29
  preserves
    in Noodle Pudding I, 126
    in Noodle Pudding II,
      127
    in Rugelach, 6
Avocados, in guacamole,
  186

Babka, Aunt Bessie's, 16
Baking Powder Biscuits,
  178
Banana(s)
  Cream Pie, 155
  in peanut butter
    sandwich, 73
Barbecued Chicken,
  Oven-, 175
Beef. *See also* Brisket
  ground, in Stuffed
    Cabbage, 153–54
  short ribs, *See* Flanken
Beets, in borscht, 9
Biscuits
  Baking Powder, 178
  Ginger, 130
  for Salmon Pie, 115–16
Blintzes, Cheese, with
  Blueberry Sauce, 14–15
Blue cheese, in Campbell's
  Cream of Tomato Soup, 64

Bologna Sandwich, The
  Perfect Jewish, 65
Borscht
  Cold (Meatless), 9
  creamy, 9
Bread(s). *See also* Biscuits;
  Coffee cake(s);
  Doughnuts
  Babka, Aunt Bessie's, 16
  Challa, 26
  crumbs, for Skillet Fried
    Chicken, 173
  egg (Challa), 26
  French Toast, 27
  Pudding, Brandied,
    12–13
  Raisin Gingerbread, 179
Bris, 134–40
  Honey Cake I, 141
  Honey Cake II, 142
Brisket, 100
  Sandwich, The Best, 101
Buttermilk
  in biscuits for Salmon
    Pie, 115–16
  Cake Doughnuts, 82

Cabbage
  Soup, Sweet-and-Sour, 29
  Stuffed, 153–54
Cake(s). *See also* Coffee
  cake(s); Frosting(s) and
  icing(s)
  Cherry, Leah's, 148–49
  Chocolate Sour Cream,
    Three-Layer, with Fudge
    Frosting, 158–59
  Doughnuts, Buttermilk,
    82
  Honey, I, 141
  Honey, II, 142
  Lemon Sponge, 30
Candied Sweet Potatoes, 55
Cannoli, 39–40
Casseroles
  Cabbage, Stuffed, 153–54
  Salmon Pie, 115–16
Challa, 26

Chanukah, 97–99
  Brisket, 100
    Sandwich, The Best,
      101
  Potato Latkes, 102
Cheddar
  in Tomato Soup,
    Campbell's Cream of, 63
  on Tuna Melt, 66
Cheese. *See also names of
  individual types of cheese*
  in Apricot Jell-O Mold,
    128
  Blintzes, with Blueberry
    Sauce, 14–15
  in Cannoli, 39–40
  in frostings and icings
    fluffy cherry, 149
    ginger cream cheese,
      179
  Grilled, Sandwich, 62
  in Italian Harvest Soup,
    206
  in Noodle Pudding I, 126
  in Noodle Pudding II,
    127
  Pie, 37–38
  on potatoes
    Baked Stuffed, 177
    Skins with Baked Eggs,
      108
  in Rugelach dough, 6
  in Tomato Soup,
    Campbell's Cream of,
    63, 64
  on Tuna Melt, 66
Cherry Cake, Leah's,
  148–49
Cherry icing, fluffy, for
  Leah's Cherry Cake, 149
Chestnuts, glacéed, in
  Nesselrode Pie, 160–61
Chicken
  Barbecued, Oven-, 175
  coatings for
    bread crumb, for Skillet
      Fried, 173
    cornflake, for Oven-
      Fried, 174

209

Chicken (cont.)
  rendering, 48–49
  skimming, from soup,
    193
  fried
    in the oven, 174
    in the skillet, 173
  liver, chopped, 96
  marinade, for Oven-
    Fried, 174
  Soup, 193–94
Chocolate
  Cake, Three-Layer Sour
    Cream, with Fudge
    Frosting, 158–59
  Coffee Frappe, 67
  frosting, *See* Fudge
    frosting Pudding, The
    World's Most Delicious,
    190
Chopped Liver, Millie's, 96
Christmas, 162–66
  Springerle, 167
Coconut Macaroons, 133
Coffee cake(s)
  Babka, Aunt Bessie's, 16
  Raspberry Streusel,
    87–88
  sour cream (babka), 16
Coffee Frappe, Chocolate,
  67
Condiments
  Applesauce, 90
  Peaches, Broiled, with
    Ginger and Brown
    Sugar, 92
  Raspberry Applesauce,
    91
Cookies and bars
  Coconut Macaroons, 133
  Ginger Biscuits, 130
  Mandlbroyt, 131–32
  Oatmeal-Raisin, 74
  Rugelach, 6–7
  Springerle, 167
Cornflake coating, for
  Oven-Fried Chicken, 174
Cornmeal, in Indian
  Pudding, 182
Cottage cheese
  in Noodle Pudding I, 126
  in Noodle Pudding II,
    127
Cream, Raspberries and,
  86
Cream cheese
  in Apricot Jell-O Mold,
    128
  in Cheese Blintzes with
    Blueberry Sauce, 14
  in frostings and icings
    fluffy cherry, 149
    ginger, 179
  in Noodle Pudding II,
    127
  in Rugelach dough, 6

Creamed Spinach with
  Toasted Pine Nuts, 189
Cream of Tomato Soup
  Campbell's, garnishes for
    63–64
  Homemade, 61
Crème Brûlée, 188
Crepes, for blintzes, 14
Croutons
  garlic, 206
  in Tomato Soup,
    Campbell's Cream of,
    64
Crumb(s)
  bread, for Skillet Fried
    Chicken, 173
  cornflake, for Oven-Fried
    Chicken, 174
  graham cracker
    for Banana Cream Pie
      crust, 155
    for Key Lime Pie crust,
      157
    for Nesselrode Pie
      crust, 160
  topping, for Deep-Dish
    Apple Pie, 56
Crust(s). *See also* Pastry
  for Cheese Pie, 37
  graham cracker, for
    Banana Cream Pie, 155
  graham cracker and
    chocolate wafer
    for Key Lime Pie, 157
    for Nesselrode pie, 160
  matzo meal, for dragonfly
    (lemon curd) tart, 199
Custard. *See* Pudding(s)
  and custard(s)

Dairy. *See* Buttermilk;
  Cheese; Cream, heavy;
  Pudding(s) and custard(s);
  Sour cream; Yogurt
Desserts. *See also* Cake(s);
  Cookies and bars; Ice
  cream; *names of individual
  fruits*; Pie(s); Pudding(s)
  and custard(s)
  Apple Strudel, 117
  Broiled Peaches with
    Ginger and Brown
    Sugar, 92
  Cannoli, 39–40
  Peach Parfait with
    Raspberry Sauce, 93
  Tart, Dragonfly, Irene
    Pletka's (Lemon Curd
    Passover Tart), 199–200
Doughnuts
  Buttermilk Cake, 82
  Raised, 80–81
Dragonfly Tart, Irene
  Pletka's (Lemon Curd
  Passover Tart),
    199–200

Egg(s). *See also* Pudding(s)
  and custard(s)
  Baked, Potato Skins with,
    108
  bread (Challa), 26
  French Toast, 27
  hard-cooked
    in egg salad, 124
    in Salmon Salad, 125
    in Tomato Soup,
      Campbell's Cream of,
      63
  in the Nest, 28
  noodles
    in Kasha Varnishkes, 10
    in Noodle Pudding I,
      126
    in Noodle Pudding II,
      127
  salad, 124

Farmer cheese
  in Cheese Blintzes with
    Blueberry Sauce, 14
  in Noodle Pudding II,
    127
Filling(s)
  for Apple Strudel, 117
  banana custard, for
    Banana Cream Pie, 155
  beef, ground, for Stuffed
    Cabbage, 153–54
  cheese
    for blintzes, 14
    for Cannoli, 40
    for Cheese Pie, 37–38
  for Key Lime Pie, 157
  lemon curd, for
    dragonfly tart, 199
  for Nesselrode Pie,
    160–61
  raisin-walnut, for
    Rugelach, 6
Fish
  Gefilte, 197
  Herring Salad, 8
  liquid for cooking, 197
  Salmon
    Pie, 115–16
    Salad, 125
  Tuna Fish Sandwich, A
    Premier, 66
  Tuna Melt, 66
Flanken
  in Cabbage Soup, Sweet-
    and-Sour, 29
  Stewed, Split Pea Soup
    with, 25
Frappe, Chocolate Coffee,
  67
Freezing, 86, 89
French Toast, 27
Frosting(s) and icing(s)
  cherry, fluffy, for Leah's
    Cherry Cake, 149
  fudge, for Three-Layer

Chocolate Sour Cream
Cake, 159
ginger cream cheese, 179
glaze, for Raspberry
Streusel Coffee Cake, 88
Fruits, glacéed, in
Nesselrode Pie, 160–61.
*See also names of
individual fruits*

Gefilte Fish, 197
Horseradish for, 198
Ginger
Biscuits, 130
and Brown Sugar, Broiled
Peaches with, 92
cream cheese icing, 179
Gingerbread, Raisin, 179
Glacéed chestnuts and
fruits, in Nesselrode Pie,
160–61
Glaze, for Raspberry
Streusel Coffee Cake, 88
Grape-Nut Pudding, 187
Grapes, in Waldorf Salad,
156
Grilled Cheese Sandwich,
62
Ground beef, in Stuffed
Cabbage, 153–54
Guacamole, Sam's, 186

Hazelnuts
in Mandlbroyt, 131–32
toasting and skinning,
132
Herring Salad, 8
Holidays and rituals. *See*
Bris; Chanukah;
Christmas; Passover;
Sitting shivah;
Thanksgiving;
Yom Kippur
Hommus, 185
Honey Cake I, 141
Honey Cake II, 142
Horseradish, 198

Ice cream
in Chocolate Coffee
Frappe, 67
Indian Pudding and, 182
Peaches, Broiled, with
Ginger and Brown
Sugar and, 92
Peach Parfait with
Raspberry Sauce and,
93
Icings. *See* Frosting(s) and
icing(s)
Indian Pudding, 182
Italian Harvest Soup, 206

Jell-O Mold, Apricot,
128–29

Kasha Varnishkes, 10
Key Lime Pie, 157
Kugel, Potato, 11

Latkes, Potato, 102
Leah's Cherry Cake, 148–49
Lemon(s)
curd Passover (dragonfly)
tart, 199–200
Limeade, 72
Sponge Cake, 30
Lime(s)
in Lemon Limeade, 72
Pie, Key, 157
Liver, Millie's Chopped, 96

Macaroons, Coconut, 133
Mandlbroyt, 131-32
Matzo
Balls I, 195
Balls II, 196
crust, for dragonfly
(lemon curd Passover)
tart, 199
Meat(s)
beef, ground, in Stuffed
Cabbage, 153–54
Brisket, 100
Flanken
Stewed, with Split Pea
Soup, 25
in Sweet-and-Sour
Cabbage Soup, 29
Milk shake. *See* Frappe,
Chocolate Coffee
Mold(s)
Apricot Jell-O, 128–29
for Springerle, 167
unmolding Jell-O, 128–29
Monterey Jack
on Potato Skins with
Baked Eggs, 108
in Tomato Soup,
Campbell's Cream of, 63

Nesselrode Pie, 160–61
Noodle(s)
in Kasha Varnishkes, 10
Pudding I, 126
Pudding II, 127
Tomato Sauce for, 36
Nuts. *See also* Almond(s);
Chestnuts, glacéed, in
Nesselrode Pie; Hazelnuts;
Pecans, in Oatmeal-Raisin
Cookies; Pine nuts;
Walnuts
freezing, 132
toasting, 38, 132

Oatmeal-Raisin Cookies,
74
Oven-Barbecued Chicken,
175
Oven-Fried Chicken, 174

Parfait, Peach, with
Raspberry Sauce, 93
Passover, 191–92
Chicken Soup, 193–94
Dragonfly Tart, Irene
Pletka's (Lemon Curd
Passover Tart), 199–200
Gefilte Fish, 197
Horseradish, 198
Lemon Curd Tart, 199–200
Matzo Balls I, 195
Matzo Balls II, 196
Pasta, Tomato Sauce for,
36. *See also* Noodle(s)
Pastry. *See also* Crust(s);
Doughnuts for Apple
Strudel, 117–18
Cannoli shells, 39–40
Pea Soup, Split, with
Stewed Flanken, 25
Peach(es)
Broiled, with Ginger and
Brown Sugar, 92
freezing, 89
Parfait with Raspberry
Sauce, 93
Peanut Butter and Banana
Sandwiches, 73
Pie(s). *See also* Crust(s);
Dragonfly Tart, Irene
Pletka's
Apple, Deep-Dish, 56
Banana Cream, 155
Cheese, 37–38
Key Lime, 157
Nesselrode, 160–61
Salmon, 115–16
Pine nuts
in Cheese Pie, 37–38
in creamed spinach, 189
toasting, 38
Potato(es)
Baked Stuffed, 177
with Brisket, 100
fried (Chips), 48–49
Kugel, 11
Latkes, 102
Mashed, 176
Skins with Baked Eggs,
108
Sweet, Candied, 55
Pudding(s) and custard(s).
See also Kugel, Potato
banana custard filling,
for pie, 155
Bread, Brandied, 12–13
Chocolate, The World's
Most Delicious, 190
cornmeal (Indian), 182
Crème Brûlée, 188
Grape-Nut, 187
Indian, 182
Noodle, I, 126
Noodle, II, 127
Rice, Creamy, 183

Raised Doughnuts, 80–81
Raspberry(ies)
  Applesauce, 91
  and Cream, 86
  freezing, 86
  Jell-O, for Apricot Jell-O
    Mold, 128
  Sauce
    Peach Parfait with, 93
    Quick, 93
  Streusel Coffee Cake,
    87–88
Rice Pudding, Creamy, 183
Ricotta
  in Cannoli filling, 40
  in Cheese Pie filling,
    37–38
  in Noodle Pudding II, 127
Rugelach, 6–7

Salad(s)
  egg, 124
  Herring, 8
  Salmon, 125
  tuna fish, 66
  Waldorf, 156
Salmon
  Pie, 115–16
  Salad, 125
Sandwiches. *See also*
    Spreads and dips
  Bologna, The Perfect
    Jewish, 65
  Brisket, The Best, 101
  Cheese, Grilled, 62
  Egg Salad, My, 124
  Peanut Butter and
    Banana, 73
  Tuna Fish, A Premier, 66
  Tuna Melt, 66
Sauce(s). *See also*
    Topping(s)
  barbecue, for Oven-
    Barbecued Chicken,
    175
  Blueberry, Cheese
    Blintzes with, 14–15
  Ginger and Brown Sugar,
    Broiled Peaches with, 92
  Raspberry, Quick, 93
  Tomato, 36
    for Stuffed Cabbage, 153
Sitting shivah, 119–23
Soup(s)
  beet (borscht), 9
  borscht
    Cold (Meatless), 9
    creamy, 9

Cabbage, Sweet-and-
    Sour, 29
  Chicken, 193–94
  croutons, garlic, for, 206
  fish stock, for Salmon
    Pie, 115
  Italian Harvest, 206
  Matzo Balls I for, 195
  Matzo Balls II for, 196
  Split Pea, with Stewed
    Flanken, 25
  Tomato, Cream of
    Campbell's, garnishes
      for, 63–64
    Homemade, 61
Sour cream
  in Apricot Jell-O Mold,
    128–29
  in borscht, creamy, 9
  Cake, Three-Layer
    Chocolate, with Fudge
    Frosting, 158–59
  in Cheese Blintzes with
    Blueberry Sauce, 14–15
  in coffee cake
    Babka, Aunt Bessie's, 16
    Streusel, Raspberry, 87
  in fudge frosting, 159
  in Noodle Pudding I,
    126
  in Noodle Pudding II,
    127
  with Potato Latkes, 102
  in Tomato Soup,
    Campbell's Cream of,
    63
  in Waldorf Salad, 156
Spinach, Creamed, with
  Toasted Pine Nuts, 189
Split Pea Soup with Stewed
  Flanken, 25
Sponge Cake, Lemon, 30
Spreads and dips
  Chopped Liver, Millie's,
    96
  Egg Salad, My, 124
  Guacamole, Sam's, 186
  Herring Salad, 8
  Hommus, 185
  Horseradish, 198
  Salmon Salad, 125
Springerle, 167
Squash, Baked Acorn,
    184
Streusel, Raspberry, Coffee
  Cake, 87–88
Strudel, Apple, 117–18
Stuffed Cabbage, 153–54

Sweet-and-Sour Cabbage
    Soup, 29
Sweet Potatoes, Candied, 55
Swiss cheese
  in Tomato Soup,
    Campbell's Cream of,
    63
  on Tuna Melt, 66

Tangerines, in Waldorf
    Salad, 156
Tart, dragonfly (lemon
  curd Passover), 199–200
Thanksgiving, 50–54
  Apple Pie, Deep-Dish,
    56
  Sweet Potatoes, Candied,
    55
Tomato(es)
  Sauce, 36
    for Stuffed Cabbage,
      153
  Soup, Cream of
    Campbell's, garnishes
      for, 63–64
    Homemade, 61
Topping(s). *See also*
    Frosting(s) and icing(s);
    Glaze, for Raspberry
    Streusel Coffee Cake;
    Sauce(s); Spreads and
    dips
  almond and apricot, for
    Noodle Pudding II, 127
  for Bread Pudding,
    Brandied, 13
  crumb, for Deep-Dish
    Apple Pie, 56
  for ice cream. *See* Ice
    cream for Key Lime
    Pie, 157
  streusel, for raspberry
    coffee cake, 87
Tuna
  Fish Sandwich, A
    Premier, 66
  Melt, 66

Varnishkes, Kasha, 10
Velveeta
  in Grilled Cheese
    Sandwich, 62
  in Italian Harvest Soup,
    206

Waldorf Salad, 156

Yom Kippur, 1–5